Which cowboy will become the first daddy in Cactus, Texas?

Their moms want grandchildren—
and these conniving matchmakers will
stop at nothing to turn their cowboy
sons into family men!
Who'll be the first to fall?

Cal Baxter
or
Spence Hauk
or
Tuck Langford
or
Mac Gibbons

4 TOTS for 4 TEXANS

Dear Reader,

After the Randalls, I didn't think I'd find four men as lovable, or hardheaded, as those cowboys. But as I turned to my native Texas for inspiration, lo and behold, there they were. Not brothers, but best friends for life.

Cal, Spence, Tuck and Mac grew up together in a small west Texas town. Oil on their family properties could have made it easy for them, but they've worked hard all their lives. They know the value of work...and friendship. Nothing can come between them, especially women. In fact, they'd vowed long ago not to marry. Or to kiss girls, either, but Tuck dismissed that promise when he was thirteen. It didn't take the others long to agree. Their bodies hardened by a tough, outdoor life, their eyes keen, their hearts filled with loyalty and honesty, these four draw women the way pie on a hot summer day draws flies.

But their mothers, with only one chick apiece, want grandchildren. The other ladies in town have babies to cuddle. Why don't they? And they set out to do something about it.

I hope you enjoy these four guys and their fall for four special women. I certainly did. But don't you stampede to Texas looking for men like these. They may be out there, but we Texas ladies aren't looking to give them away!

Judy Christenberry

Daddy Unknown

JUDY CHRISTENBERRY

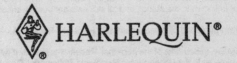

HARLEQUIN®

TORONTO • NEW YORK • LONDON
AMSTERDAM • PARIS • SYDNEY • HAMBURG
STOCKHOLM • ATHENS • TOKYO • MILAN • MADRID
PRAGUE • WARSAW • BUDAPEST • AUCKLAND

ISBN 0-373-16781-4

DADDY UNKNOWN

Copyright © 1999 by Judy Russell Christenberry

This edition published by arrangement with Harlequin Books S.A.

Look us up on-line at: http://www.romance.net

Printed in U.S.A.

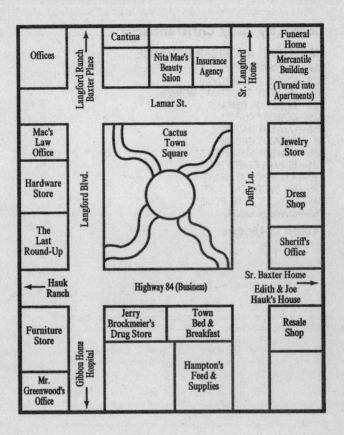

Books by Judy Christenberry

HARLEQUIN AMERICAN ROMANCE

Prologue

"I can't believe it!" Mabel Baxter exclaimed as she pushed the deck of cards toward Edith Hauk, who was sitting on her left.

"Oh, come on, Mabel," Florence Gibbons said with a grin. "You've lost before. Remember when you bid five spades and—"

"Of course I've lost at cards. That's not what I'm upset about." The disgust in her voice caught everyone's attention.

Ruth Langford didn't look up. "Serves you right. You were so sure you'd already won." It was the first time in several weeks the four of them had discussed their bet of who would get the first grandbaby.

"Well, at least mine got married," Mabel returned, her jaw clenched.

"But you still don't have a grandbaby!" Ruth reminded her, glaring.

"Girls, girls, girls," Florence chided gently. "We're friends. Always have been and always will be. Let's not try to hurt each other."

"You're right," Mabel said with a sigh. "Sorry, Ruth. Tuck will find someone. He's a good boy."

Ruth nodded her thanks, but her mind was on her son. "He used to be. Then he went kind of wild about the time Spence and Melanie married. Now I think he's depressed. He never goes anywhere—except for the Saturdays he spends with the boys. I'm worried about him."

Florence admitted with a sigh, "At least he's ahead of Mac."

"What do you mean?" Ruth asked.

"Tuck has shown he's human. Mac doesn't get close to any woman. For any reason! I'm beginning to worry about him."

The other three women gasped.

"You don't mean you think—" Mabel stopped, unable to give voice to her thought.

Florence's cheeks flushed. "No! At least— I don't know. I'm...concerned." She kept her gaze fixed on her hands, squeezed tightly together on the table.

"I don't believe it," Edith said firmly. "He's just made up his mind, and he's always been a stubborn little cuss. But I've seen him looking." She grinned at Florence. "He definitely looks."

"Looking won't get me a grandbaby."

"Well, I can guarantee you mine is doing more than looking," Mabel said, "but I'm not getting a grandbaby, either."

"Me, neither," Edith said. "I thought maybe Melanie had gained a little weight. When I asked Spence, he laughed and warned me not to say anything. He said he and Maria were conspiring to fat-ten her up. The doctor said she needed to gain weight.''

"Maybe she *is* pregnant and they're just not telling you," Ruth suggested, a struggle visible on her face as she tried to look happy.

"No. It's only been two months. That wouldn't be enough time to be *that* pregnant, and Spence isn't that good an actor."

"I think maybe I need to talk to Doc," Ruth suddenly said, her lips firming.

"To Doc? Are you sick?" Florence asked.

"No. I mean talk to him about Tuck. Maybe see if he thinks my boy is depressed. They got drugs for those things these days, you know."

"Do they have drugs to make women pregnant?" Mabel asked.

"Why not? They've got that Viagra for old goats who should know better," Ruth answered.

"Then maybe I'll talk to him about Jessica," Mabel said.

"And I'll talk to him about Melanie," Edith added, nodding her head.

"Well, I'm not going to be the only one who doesn't use modern science," Florence said. "I'm making an appointment first thing in the morning."

Chapter One

Saturday night.

Tuck looked at the attractive faces around his table. He'd tried to feel good about being here with his friends. He'd tried to forget the changes in his life. He'd tried to forget her.

But he couldn't.

Hell, he'd worked real hard to find a substitute for her. And there had been more than a few volunteers. Even the most willing hadn't interested him. Maybe he needed to see Doc.

"Something wrong with your steak, Tuck?" Jessica Baxter, Cal's wife and restaurant owner, asked.

He looked down at his almost full plate. Then he tried a smile for Jess. "Nah, it's perfect, as usual. Guess I didn't work hard enough today to have an appetite."

"You hung on that old bull for the full eight seconds," Spencer Hauk, another of his old friends and the latest newlywed, reminded him.

His wife, Melanie, shuddered. "He was so mean."

"Tuck?" Spence asked with a grin. "Nah, he's not that bad."

Melanie blushed. "Of course I didn't mean Tuck. I meant the bull."

Amid the laughter at Spence's teasing, Tuck sipped his beer. Then he grimaced. Even beer didn't offer him any relief. He waved to Nita, their waitress. "Would you bring me a glass of tea, Nita?"

Cal frowned. "You tired of beer?"

"It's getting warm. I thought I'd get something cool," he muttered. Everyone stared at his bottle of beer, its sides frosty.

"Yeah," Mac muttered. "I think the temperature is going to top fifty tomorrow."

"Hey, it's March. A warm front could hit town any day," Tuck protested.

"And you're cooling off in advance?" Mac persisted.

Tuck gave up. With a shrug, he said, "I don't know what the hell I'm doing," he muttered.

Mac patted him on the shoulder and said nothing else.

Jessica cleared her throat. "We have some news that might cheer you up."

Tuck barely even paid any attention to her words until he noticed sudden tension in both Cal and Spence. He checked Mac's response and saw no emotion there. "What's she talking about?" he asked.

"I don't know," Mac said.

"You're the only two who don't know," Spence said.

"Know what?" Mac asked.

Spence put his arm around Melanie, cuddling her against him, and Cal did the same to Jessica. Tuck narrowed his gaze. "Wait a minute. It's the baby thing, isn't it?"

"'The baby thing?'" Mac repeated. Then it hit him. "You're expecting? Both of you?" he asked the ladies.

They both nodded, then shushed Mac as he whooped.

"Why is that good news for *us?*" Tuck asked. "I mean, I'm happy for the four of you, but—"

"Don't you get it? My aunt Florence and your mother won't be worrying about finding us wives," Mac assured him. "We're home free." Mac grinned at him, relief on his handsome face.

Tuck stared at him blankly. "Oh. Oh, yeah."

Mac stared at him. "You change your mind about marriage?"

At one time, the four men, Cal, Spence, Mac and Tuck had been united in their determination to remain bachelors. Then Cal had realized he loved Jessica, a lifelong friend, and Spence had suddenly married Melanie almost two months ago.

Tuck shrugged his shoulders. "Nope. I don't think marriage is for me." He realized how gloomy he sounded when his friends had just given them good news. "Mac and I will be great uncles to your children. Do you know if they're boys or girls? And, hey, who's going to win the contest?"

Melanie's cheeks flushed, but she gamely answered. "We still don't know."

"Why not?" Mac asked, frowning. "I mean you

and Spence got married two months after— I mean—''

Spence cleared his throat. ''Well, it's hard to—''

''No, it's not,'' Cal said. He looked at his two bachelor friends. ''We both got pregnant on the same day, our wedding day. At least we think so.''

Tuck wasn't quite clear how they could be sure, but when Cal opened his mouth to further explain, Jessica intervened.

''Just take our word for it. So we still don't know who will win, but I guess your parents will give up trying to win since it takes nine months for a baby, whenever you start.'' After a moment of silence, she added, ''We thought you'd be happy.''

Tuck nodded, trying to smile, but he was thinking about Jessica and Cal's wedding day. He'd been happy for his friends, but he'd been happier for himself. The day had ended in a blaze of glory, holding her in his arms, loving her, never wanting to let her go.

''Hey, have you told Alex yet?'' Mac asked, grinning.

Tuck knocked over his discarded beer and everyone jumped back from the table. He gathered napkins and tried to mop up the mess. Nita came running, a cup towel in her hands.

When the spill had been cleaned up and Nita had departed, everyone settled back down at the table.

''Sorry,'' Tuck muttered. Nita returned with a glass of iced tea for him and asked if anyone else needed something. When she'd left, Mac repeated his question.

''No, we haven't told anyone. We're each going

to tell our parents tomorrow and then I'll call Alex,'' Jessica said. ''I haven't talked to her since, well, I guess it's been at least several months. I know it was before your wedding, Melanie.''

''I'm sure it was. Edith tried to call her about our wedding, but she never got hold of her.''

Tuck already knew all that. He'd even driven to Dallas to talk to Alex, the beautiful blond attorney who'd helped Jessica with the sale of her Mexican restaurants.

Because he'd become more than friends with Alex.

Fool that he was, he'd actually even considered following his friends down the aisle. That thought brought actual pain to his chest. He should've known better. Alex was a sophisticated lawyer, living in Dallas. He was a rancher, living in Cactus, Texas, a small west Texas town northwest of Lubbock.

But she'd melted like warm honey in his arms. And he couldn't forget her.

He also couldn't find her. Or, at least, the last time he'd tried, about the time of the second wedding. She'd gone out of town on a case. He'd left message after message, but she'd never returned his calls. He'd driven to Dallas two weekends in a row, but she didn't come home. He'd even weaseled the name of her hotel in D.C. from her secretary, but she hadn't returned that call, either.

He might be arrogant, as she'd once said, but he wasn't stupid. He didn't have to be hit on the head with a two-by-four to know she was tired of her cowboy, as she'd called him.

Besides, she'd already been…unhappy. She'd assured him it wasn't him, but for the first time he'd lacked the assurance he'd had with other women. Alex was different. And he'd wanted her with his entire being.

Then he'd gotten angry.

How could she throw away what they'd had? They could've worked something out. Hell, for Alex, he'd even considered moving to a larger town, away from his beloved ranch.

"Tuck?" Jessica asked. "Have you talked to Alex lately?"

"No!" he almost shouted. Pulling himself under control, he added, "Why would I have?"

No one answered, but he intercepted several sympathetic looks. Hell, everyone knew. He wasn't fooling anyone. Jumping to his feet, he muttered his goodbyes, but Mac stood and put a hand on his shoulder.

"Hold on, Tuck. We understand."

Tuck fell back into his chair and covered his eyes with his hands.

"Have some iced tea," Melanie suggested softly, pushing his glass a little closer.

"Yeah," Cal agreed, "before you spill it all over us."

Jessica protested, "Cal!"

"Do you think this guy gave me any sympathy in my misery? Hell, no!" Cal was studying his friend with a grin.

Tuck glared at him. "I teased a little. That's all."

Cal nodded. "I know, buddy. I was just giving you time to pull yourself together."

"Thanks." Tuck sucked in a deep breath and tried to change the subject. "You know, I think I've worked up an appetite now." He picked up his knife and fork and cut off a slice of his steak. As he chewed what tasted like sawdust, his friends began speculating on their parents' reaction to their news.

Then he looked up.

And thought he was seeing a ghost.

Or at least one of his vivid dreams.

Alexandra Logan, lawyer extraordinaire, from the big city of Dallas, was standing in the foyer of The Last Roundup.

ALEXANDRA LOGAN PAUSED before she entered the restaurant in the small Texas town. Would she find answers here? This was her last hope. She closed her eyes, wrapping her arms around her body, shivering in spite of the jacket she wore.

"You okay, Ms. Logan?" Bill Parker asked from behind her. He was the P.I. she'd finally hired last week to help her put her life back together. If that was possible.

"Are you sure this is the right place?"

"Yes, ma'am. At the time you were here, Ms. Hoya was selling a string of Mexican restaurants. But this is her latest project. The Last Roundup. And she married. Now she's Jessica Baxter. I believe you came to her wedding."

When she still didn't move or speak, he prodded, "Do you remember?"

She shook her head, her eyes still closed.

"Do you want to go in here? There wasn't anyone at their home."

She couldn't speak. Licking her suddenly dry lips, she nodded and opened her eyes. Still she couldn't move. The gray-haired detective took her arm and urged her up the steps.

They walked into the brightly lit foyer, engulfed with chatter and music as soon as the doors opened. She felt herself withdrawing, something the once forthright, confident Alex would never have done. She'd embraced life.

But no longer.

A charming young woman greeted them. "Good evening. Will there be two for dinner?"

Bill stepped forward when Alex didn't speak. "Yeah. Uh, by the way, is the owner here this evening? Jessica Baxter?"

"Yes, she is. Did you want to speak to her?"

"Yes, please."

"Follow me. I'll take you by her table before I seat you," the hostess said cheerfully.

Bill took Alex's arm and steered her after the hostess. But suddenly her way was impeded by a tall, rugged, cowboy-to-die-for.

"What are you doing here?" he growled.

Alex stared at him. As far as she knew, she'd never seen him before in her life.

Then she was surrounded by several people and a beautiful black-haired woman was hugging her.

"Alex, it's great to see you!"

TUCK HAD GOTTEN UP from the table without a word to his friends. He hadn't even remembered them. All he'd seen was Alex, his beautiful Alex.

But he hadn't been able to hide his anger. After all, she'd put him through hell.

Shoved aside by Jessica, he stood back, his hungry eyes taking in her sophisticated image. His eyes narrowed. Something was different. What was going on?

"Hello," Alex said, her voice hesitant.

Jessica released her, a puzzled look on her face. "Are you all right?"

"Yes, of course." She smiled, but Tuck thought she looked nervous. Her smile, like a hundred-watt bulb, was something he'd always enjoyed about her, but it was not so bright this evening.

"You're probably tired from the drive. Come join us. Cal, find Nita," Jessica ordered as she took Alex's arm.

Tuck moved to her other side, dying to touch her. He came to an abrupt halt as an older, gray-haired man took her other arm.

"Oh, I'm sorry, I didn't know—" Jessica said, staring at the man. "I thought you were alone," she added to Alex.

Freezing, Tuck stared at the man, anger building within him. She'd brought some man to throw in his face? How could she be so cruel?

He had actually turned away, heading for the door, when he caught Alex's explanation.

"This is Bill Parker. He...he's a private investigator."

Tuck spun on his boot heel, glowering at the man still holding Alex's arm.

His friends all looked at each other. Well, if they weren't going to ask the damn question, he would.

"Why?"

She looked at him, her eyes wide. "Why what?"

"Why do you have a private investigator?"

He hated it when her gaze moved to the older man, as if he would speak for her.

"Ms. Logan has experienced some difficulties in recent months and needed—"

"What difficulties?" Tuck snapped.

The detective looked around. "Would it be possible for us to sit down? The explanation is rather lengthy."

Jessica, ever the hostess, assured the man that of course they could sit down. She led the way back to the big round table they usually used, asking Cal to pull up a couple more chairs. Everyone shifted their place settings to leave enough room for the new pair.

Tuck made sure he was sitting next to Alex, on her right, even though the other man stuck to her like glue, on her left.

Jessica flagged down Nita to order food and drink for her new guests, even though Alex protested that she couldn't eat.

"I think you'd better, Ms. Logan. You scarcely ate any lunch," the man said in a soft voice.

Tuck wouldn't have heard him if he hadn't been watching him like a hawk. He turned to stare at Alex again and thought she looked tired, almost faded, compared to the brilliant beauty who had captivated him months ago.

"Are you sick?" he demanded, his voice hard as fear filled him.

Startled, she stared at him, looking like a deer caught in the headlights. "N-no."

"And who might you be?" Bill Parker said, leaning forward.

Tuck squared his shoulders. "Tucker Langford."

"Ah." He shot a look at Alex that made Tuck want to punch his lights out.

"What does 'ah' mean?" he questioned, glaring at the man.

"You called Ms. Logan several times."

"Damn right I did. Not that she bothered to answer." His gaze switched to Alex, but she kept her head down.

"Would one of you please tell us what's happened?" Jessica asked.

Parker looked at Alex, but she didn't look up. Finally he said, "Ms. Logan was in an accident in D.C. While working on a case there."

Everyone expressed concern except Tuck. He couldn't speak. The thought that he might have lost Alex forever made it almost impossible to breathe.

"She hit her head and experienced amnesia." Parker held up his hand as several people started to ask questions. "The doctor thinks she will make a full recovery eventually, but there are circumstances that make it imperative that she recover her life now."

"What circumstances?" Cal asked. As the sheriff of their little town, he liked to have all the details.

Before Bill Parker could speak, Alex put her hand on his arm and took a deep breath.

"What Bill is trying to say as delicately as possible is…I'm pregnant and I don't know who the daddy is."

Chapter Two

"That baby had damn well better be mine," Tuck said, his tone explosive as he broke the stunned silence around the table.

"You and Alex—" Jessica began, then broke off.

"Mr. Langford!" Bill Parker leaned forward.

"You?" Alex said, a surprised look on her face.

"Why are you surprised?" Tuck demanded, leaning toward her.

She pulled back, brushing against her private detective, waiting for any sense of recognition. How could she have made love with this man and have no memory of it?

"Well?" Tuck persisted.

"Because...because I can't remember." She could tell he didn't like her answer. She didn't blame him. He was totally unforgettable...in most circumstances.

"You don't remember anything?" he asked, his voice rising.

The man beside him took his arm, and the man who seemed attached to the dark-haired woman who had hugged her urged him to back off.

Alex scooted her chair a little closer to Bill Parker. She hadn't met him until after she lost her memory. This man knew her as she was. The others around the table knew her from her forgotten past. One of them claimed to have known her intimately.

Bill spoke. "Look, Mr. Langford, we appreciate your interest in this...case. But you have to understand that Ms. Logan remembers nothing. It has nothing to do with you, any of you. We're trying to figure out what happened the past few months. And we'd appreciate your help."

The man called Tuck looked at Bill, his jaw clenched, his gaze stormy. But he nodded his head.

Alex took a deep breath. "I—I apologize, but could each of you introduce yourself to me? I'm feeling a little lost."

The dark-haired woman smiled. "Of course. I'm Jessica Hoya Baxter. We first met when I contacted your firm in Dallas about handling negotiations for my Mexican restaurants."

"I read the file," Alex said, nodding.

Jessica smiled. "You did a great job. And...and we became friends. You returned for a party at Tuck's ranch a few weeks later."

"And the wedding?" Alex had found charges for a wedding present and for gasoline purchases from Dallas to Cactus.

"Yes, you returned for our wedding."

After that, they went around the table, introducing themselves until they reach Tucker Langford. He turned to glare at her. "We became lovers."

He didn't appear to be happy about that fact. Neither was she, for that matter. It certainly complicated her life.

She had a lot of questions she wanted answered, but not in front of an audience.

"So the baby is mine. Case solved," he added, looking at Bill Parker.

"Not exactly," the detective said with a sigh. Alex knew what was coming and wished she could run away.

"You see," Bill continued, "you're not the only one claiming to be the father of Ms. Logan's baby."

TUCK THOUGHT he was going to lose what little he'd eaten. The thought that Alex had been sleeping with someone else while they'd— No! He refused to believe it.

"Who?" Cal asked. "Who is claiming to be the father?"

"A lawyer in Ms. Logan's office," the detective replied when Alex said nothing.

"Chad Lowery," Tuck muttered.

Both the detective and Alex turned to stare at him.

Her cheeks flushed, she asked, "How did you know?"

"You talked about him."

"To you?"

He nodded. When he'd given her a tour of his ranch, grateful to get her alone, he'd immediately asked if she was involved with another man. "You said you'd just broken up with Chad."

"When was that?" she asked.

"Late October."

"How far along are you?" Jessica asked.

"About four months," Alex whispered.

"Well, there you have it, then," Cal, the sheriff, said with a grin. "Congratulations, Tuck."

"Not so fast," Bill Parker said. "Mr. Lowery claims he had relations with Alex until her departure for D.C."

Pain shafted through Tuck as he stared at her. "Is that true?"

"I don't know!" she exclaimed, her voice rising. "I don't know."

Only the weariness and concern in her voice stopped Tuck from walking out. Even the thought that she had betrayed him in such a way was almost more than he could bear.

"What happens now?" Mac asked, leaning forward.

Alex sat with her head down, saying nothing.

Bill Parker shrugged his shoulders. "We're going to find a place to stay tonight, and tomorrow, we'll try to reconstruct what happened here with Ms. Logan."

"You may have to return to Lubbock, or drive on to Muleshoe to find a decent place. The bed-and-breakfast on the square is full tonight," Cal said. "They've got a bunch of writers from Amarillo staying here for the weekend."

Bill Parker frowned and looked at his client. "How far would that be to drive back to Lubbock? An hour?"

"Just about," Cal confirmed.

"Why don't you stay in my condo?" Jessica suggested. "It's empty." She bit her bottom lip. "Oh, there's only one bed, though. I moved the other to Cal's house.''

"I have a spare room," Tuck suddenly said. "Alex could stay with me and Mr. Parker could use the condo.''

It pained him when Alex's gaze widened and fear filled her eyes.

Parker spoke before she could. "If you wouldn't mind reversing that proposition, we'd be glad to accept. That would be all right with you, Ms. Logan, wouldn't it? If you stayed at the condo and I accepted Mr. Langford's gracious offer?''

Tuck wanted to protest, but Bill Parker met his gaze with resolution. Tuck accepted that the invitation would be on Parker's terms or not at all.

"Would you mind, Jessica?" Alex asked.

Her hesitancy surprised Tuck. She'd always been so sure of herself. Now there was a shyness that entranced him. But then, everything about Alex had always held his attention.

"Of course I don't mind.''

Alex nodded to her investigator.

"We appreciate your offer, Mrs. Baxter. Ms. Logan tires quickly these days." Bill Parker touched Alex's arm as he spoke.

Tuck wanted to tell him to take his hands off Alex. But the woman hadn't recognized any claim on his part. He said nothing.

"Forgive me for asking," Melanie said in a soft voice, leaning forward, "but did you say you were four months pregnant?''

Alex, her cheeks red, said, "The doctor thinks I'm approximately fifteen or sixteen weeks.''

Tuck didn't need to count the weeks. "Your wedding day," he added, nodding at Cal.

To everyone's surprise, Melanie laughed. Then Jessica, catching a look from her friend, joined in the laughter. Then Cal and Spence followed suit.

"What's so funny?" Tuck demanded in a growl.

It was Cal who answered. "The baby race, man. Don't you get it? We told you we both got pregnant on our wedding day. Now you're saying Alex did, too. Your mom is going to be ecstatic!"

EXHAUSTED and more confused than ever, Alex asked for an explanation.

Spence explained the bet their mothers had made.

"But we don't know that…that he's the father," Alex insisted. "According to the attorney at my office, this could be his baby. And even if it is Tuck's, it could've happened on another date."

"Nope," Tuck said, shaking his head. "It couldn't have."

"How do you know?" she demanded, irritation filling her.

"Because we only did it twice. The other time we used protection. On their wedding day, things—got out of control."

Mac, the lawyer at the table, looked at his friend, one eyebrow raised. "You didn't use protection?"

Alex watched as the cowboy's face reddened. Good. He sounded just a little too sure of himself, in her opinion.

Tuck firmed his lips and stared at the center of his table, shaking his head no.

"Didn't I ask you to?" she said, knowing without

being able to remember that protection would be important to her, and wondering if he'd been too macho to do what she asked. Some men were like that, and she didn't think this cowboy lacked testosterone.

She thought he wouldn't look at her, but his gaze whipped to her face, as if he had nothing to hide. "I told you things got out of control. Neither of us thought of it until it was too late."

"And you never heard from her again?" Bill Parker asked.

"We'd planned for me to come to Dallas in two weeks. But she called and canceled on me. Said she had a big case that was going to take all her time. She'd get back to me."

She could tell her cancellation had hurt him. There was anger in his tight words.

"According to what I've discovered," Bill Parker said, "she was working fourteen- and fifteen-hour days before she left for D.C., where the case was to be argued. She was working on the case with Chad Lowery, the other man who claims to be the father of her child."

That didn't lessen the tension in the man on her right. She couldn't blame him. According to Chad, the beauty of their working on the same case and traveling together was that they could be together and still get their work done.

The waitress brought their dinners. Alex had asked for milk. It wasn't until the waitress made a remark about all the women drinking milk that Alex realized Jessica and Melanie also had glasses of milk in front of them.

A feeling of sisterhood invaded her murky thoughts, an idea that comforted her and made her feel less isolated. She smiled shakily at the other two as she raised her milk glass in a salute.

Suddenly she hoped the cowboy was right, that he was the father of her baby, and that she shared a conception day with these two women.

"Can't I take a test or something, to prove that the baby's mine?" Tuck suddenly demanded.

"It's best to wait until after the baby's born," she said softly.

"But that means my kid will be born a bastard!" he exclaimed, anger in his voice.

Cal calmed him down. "But you'll be able to prove for sure that the baby's yours then. There won't be any doubt."

"I don't want to wait." He turned to stare at Alex. "We'll get married now. Then, the baby will have my name when it's born."

"No," she said calmly, though her heart was beating in her throat. "I won't marry anyone until I know who the daddy is."

"But—" Tuck began in protest.

"This will all be resolved if Ms. Logan regains her memory." Bill Parker's words brought the discussion to an abrupt end.

In the midst of the silence, Jessica leaned forward. "How can we help her?"

"The doctor said she probably wouldn't regain her memory until the stress eases. Admittedly, her being pregnant hasn't let that happen, but her caseload at her job in Dallas was heavy. The doctor has forbidden her to return to work until her memory returns.''

Alex shrugged her shoulders. ''It's not like my firm is anxious to have me before then, either.'' She hoped no one realized how dejected she felt. As far as she'd learned, her work had ruled her life. Without it, there seemed to be a gaping hole in her future as well as her past.

''What about your family?'' Mac asked. ''Did you confide in—''

''She doesn't have any,'' Tuck said before Alex could respond.

Alex looked at the fellow lawyer. ''I have a couple of cousins in Philadelphia, an elderly aunt in Pittsburgh, but that's all. No one I would have confided in.'' Her frustration rose. ''Apparently, I didn't have any close friends, either. My...my work was my life.''

Melanie said softly what Alex hadn't. ''And now you don't have it anymore. You must be feeling lost.''

Alex could only nod. If she'd tried to speak, a sob might have escaped, completely humiliating her.

''So you stay here.''

She turned to look at the speaker, the cowboy who claimed to be the father of her baby. ''What?''

''I said you should stay here. You can't work, and if you return to Dallas, all you'll be able to do is stare at the walls. You stay here, relax, get to know us all again. We were your friends. You were happy here.''

''That's a good idea,'' Jessica agreed. ''The condo is empty. It wouldn't take much to make it habitable. I can loan you linens, dishes. There's still a table and chairs in the kitchen.''

"We've got an extra television you can use," Spence said.

"Aunt Florence has a sofa she's thinking about selling. You can use it as long as you want," Mac said.

They all stared at her, waiting for her response. And she didn't know what to say. Their offer was kind. But she'd go crazy here, too, without her work. "I— Thank you, but I...don't know what to say."

"If you're worried about how to fill the time, you could work a few hours a week at my law office," Mac offered. "Nothing big, do a little research, maybe even a little filing," he added with a grin.

"You could help me with my new store," Melanie said. "It's a consignment shop. You have excellent taste. You'd be great."

"You seemed interested in ranching while you were here," Tuck said, his voice calm and reasonable for the first time. "I can show you around the ranch some more." He paused and then added, "In return, you could help me redo my kitchen."

"I don't know how to do carpentry," she said, surprised.

He grinned at her and she saw how she could've lost her heart, or at least her body, to this man.

"I didn't mean connect up the plumbing or hammer in the nails, sweetheart. I meant pick out wallpaper and stoves and all that stuff. Do you know how many choices of wallpaper there are?" His bewilderment at such a ridiculous thing brought a gur-

gle of laughter to her that had been woefully absent
since she'd woken up in the hospital in D.C.

Jessica reached over Bill Parker to squeeze her
hand. "Will you stay, Alex? Will you let us try to
help you?"

She still didn't answer. Bill Parker, the one person
she trusted, chimed in. "I think it's a good idea,
Alex. The doc said you've got to reduce your stress,
and this place, and these people, could help you."

Looking at Jessica, she said, "Are you sure you
don't mind letting me stay in the condo?"

"Of course not. Or you could live at the ranch
with us. I just thought you could use some space,
some privacy."

"Thank you," Alex said, releasing a sigh. "All
right, I'll stay."

THE TIGHTNESS in Tuck's chest uncoiled just a little
with Alex's acceptance of Jessica's offer. He believed her baby was his, and he knew he'd need time
to convince her. He also needed time to figure out
why she hadn't contacted him.

Because she had to have known she was pregnant
before she went to D.C.

Why hadn't she told him?

Could she have been sleeping with Chad as well
as him? Tuck didn't want to believe such a thing.
But even if that were true, he wasn't going to lose
his child.

So he needed time, as much as Alex did.

"Well," Jessica said, intruding on his thoughts,
"let's get you settled in. You look a little tired."

Tuck studied Alex's face. Yes, there were circles

under her eyes, and her skin was pale. "Did the doctor say everything's all right with your pregnancy?"

"Yes, of course," she answered hurriedly. A little too fast in Tuck's opinion.

"We've got a good doctor here, Doc Greenfield. We'll get you an appointment right away," he said.

"I can assure you the doctors in Dallas are quite competent."

He leaned around her and looked at the investigator. "When did she first go to the doctor?"

After a brief glance at his client, Parker answered, "When she was six weeks along."

"Before the trip to D.C.?"

"Yeah."

Coldness settled around Tuck's heart. He'd been trying to reach her then, leaving messages at home, calling the office. And she'd known she was pregnant.

Did that mean it wasn't his baby?

"Why?" He stared at her, waiting for an explanation.

"What?"

"Why didn't you tell me?"

She took a deep breath, then turned to stare at him. "Maybe because it isn't your baby. I don't really know."

He jumped to his feet, unable to calmly listen to her response. Mac stood with him, putting a hand on his shoulder.

"Don't blame her, Tuck. She doesn't remember."

"If she was sleeping with both of us at the same time, then I can blame her. She didn't have amnesia then. If she was using me for amusement, lying to me, I can blame her.'' He knew his bitterness sounded through his voice, but if she was leading him on, laughing at him with her sophisticated lawyer lover in Dallas, it would be more than he could bear.

"You won't know until she recovers her memory," Mac reminded him, "and she can't do that until the stress goes away."

Tuck heard his unspoken message. Quit causing stress. Okay, okay, he'd try to forget this woman had trampled on his heart. For now. But they were going to have a standoff once she got that memory back.

"Fine. Let's go get her settled in."

"I'll need to get some linens from my house," Jessica said. "That will take half an hour."

Cal intervened. "Why don't you just call Mom? She's five minutes away and can meet us there."

"Oh, good idea. I'll be right back."

Melanie looked at Tuck. "Do you have everything you need for Mr. Parker to stay with you? We could loan you things, or take him in ourselves."

"I've got plenty," Tuck said. "And it will kill two birds with one stone. I have some questions for Mr. Parker."

He noticed Alex seemed alarmed about him questioning her investigator, but Bill Parker didn't blink an eye. He'd be a hard nut to crack.

Jessica returned to the table. "Mabel will bring everything you'll need for tonight. Then tomorrow we'll set up household again."

"I'll have to return to Dallas anyway," Alex said.

"I only brought enough clothes for an overnight stay. And I'll need to notify some people about where I'll be."

"I'll take you to Dallas," Tuck immediately offered. And he'd keep Chad Lowery at a distance while she was there.

"Oh, no, I couldn't ask—"

"It won't be a problem. You'll need someone to carry the heavy things anyway. You shouldn't lift anything in your condition."

Bill Parker leaned forward. "I'll be going back to Dallas. I can help her."

Tuck thought fast. "I don't think she should turn around and make the drive to Dallas tomorrow, which I figure is what you're going to do. She should rest a couple of days first."

He'd scored a point, he could tell. The investigator looked at him and then Alex. Then he said, "We'll discuss it in the morning."

"Then let's go get Alex settled. You can trust us, Mr. Parker," Jessica assured the man. "I know you're anxious to find a bed, too, so you can go on with Tuck."

Tuck stood again. "That's okay. We'll be going to the condo first."

"Why?" both Jessica and Alex asked, one with curiosity and the other with alarm.

"Because I want to see if the condo brings back any memories," Tuck said.

"You mean, I've stayed there before?" Alex asked.

"You've stayed there several times," Jessica confirmed.

"No, that's not the reason," Tuck said, staring at Alex. "I want to see if you remember anything because that's where our child was conceived."

Chapter Three

Alex rode with Jessica and her husband to the condo where she was to spend the night. She was grateful to have some distance from the man claiming to have fathered her baby.

Every time she was near him, her stomach did flips. Was it sexual attraction? She could understand her sleeping with him. He was a sexy man. But she couldn't understand her sleeping with two men at once.

"Here we are," Jessica announced. "There's Mabel's car. I bet she's already got the bed made up for you."

"That would be heavenly," Alex murmured. Just thinking about a soft bed made her feel better.

She got out of the car, only to find the cowboy in her face again, waiting for her.

"I—I need to go inside," she whispered, hoping he'd let her go.

Jessica tried to intervene. "Tuck, maybe you should wait—"

"I want a word with her, Jess. I've waited four months. Just give me a minute."

Alex watched Jessica shrug her shoulders apologetically and move toward the condo. At least there were people in sight. She had no idea what this man would do.

"All right," he said gruffly, "relax. I'm not going to eat you. But I don't like discussing our personal business in front of everyone."

She shook her head. She didn't want to discuss anything with him. Period. But if what he said was true, she'd have to. "Uh, I can't remember—"

"I know. You said that." Exasperation filled his voice. "All I want is for you and me to sit down and talk face-to-face, alone, before you leave again."

"I'm not sure—"

"Damn it, I know this is my baby. You're not going to disappear on me again!"

She looked toward the condo, the porch light shining on Bill Parker and the couple who'd brought her. The cowboy clutched her shoulders, not hurting her, but making her nervous.

"You owe me that, Alex. Promise." His voice turned husky on that last word, and she felt her insides melting. Somehow, that last sound made her believe that he might be right. He might be the father of her child.

He might've been her lover.

"All right. I promise I won't leave without— without talking to you."

"In private," he insisted, seeming to want all the i's dotted and the t's crossed.

"In private," she whispered, daring to lift her gaze to his determined face.

He stepped back, releasing her, and she realized he was waiting for her to walk away, toward the others. She wasn't sure why that was such a hard task, but she hoped it had something to do with exhaustion.

It couldn't possibly be attraction for a tall, sexy cowboy.

THE SUN WARMED HER CHEEKS and Alex stretched under the covers, not quite awake, but no longer sleeping. She felt good this morning, more rested than she had in weeks. Maybe today she'd have more energy.

Her lips were stretching into a smile when reality returned. She wasn't home in her bed. She wasn't going to dress and go into the office. She didn't have her memory back.

The comfort disappeared and she felt the tension invade her mind. None of her problems had gone away. In fact, thanks to Tuck Langford, they'd doubled. She now had two men claiming to be the father of her child.

Her hand automatically stroked her expanded stomach, feeling the changes in her body. She'd had to buy a larger clothing size to accommodate her waist, but she could still hide the pregnancy from the casual observer.

Though not for much longer.

But maybe soon she'd at least know who was responsible. If she continued to sleep as well as she did last night, perhaps her memory would come back as quickly as it had gone.

She threw back the covers and wandered downstairs. Mrs. Baxter, Jessica's mother-in-law, had brought over milk and muffins last night, so she'd be able to eat when she awoke. That was exactly what she planned to do. Have a leisurely breakfast before she faced anyone or anything.

TUCK HURRIED BACK to the house, figuring his guest wouldn't be a late sleeper. He hadn't gotten a chance to ask his questions last night. Now was the right time.

Entering his kitchen, he wasn't surprised to discover Bill Parker sitting at the breakfast table, a cup of coffee in front of him. By the steam rising from the liquid, he figured the man had just come down.

"Morning. Ready for breakfast?"

"I don't want to cause any trouble," the older man said pleasantly.

Tuck was already breaking eggs into a bowl. "No problem. I waited to eat with you. I'm no Julia Child, but I can scramble eggs."

In a few minutes he set two plates of scrambled eggs and bacon, along with canned biscuits, on the table. Then he filled his own cup with coffee, refilled Parker's, and joined him at the table.

"Thanks," Parker said, nodding as he picked up his fork.

"I want to ask you some questions," Tuck said in response, only acknowledging Parker's gratitude with a nod of his head.

"I figured."

Tuck gave a half smile. This man reminded him of some of the old cowboys in the area. They never wasted words. He got down to business. "Did you interview Lowery?"

"Yeah."

"Did you believe his story?"

"No more than I believe yours."

Tuck stiffened, then relaxed again. "I'm not lying."

"He said he wasn't, either."

Taking a bite of eggs, Tuck thought about his next question. "Did you find any corroborating evidence?"

Parker stared at him. "Big word for a cowboy."

Again Tuck stiffened. Then he realized the man was testing him. "I'm a cowboy with a college degree who has a friend who's a lawyer."

Parker nodded. "Well, to tell the truth, the answer to that question is no. Alex's secretary said she knew Alex's relationship with Lowery went beyond coworkers, but she didn't know how far...or for how long."

"That would be Sylvia?"

"Right. She remembered you calling. A lot."

Tuck nodded. "Did the man act like he was happy about the baby? Like he cared about Alex?"

"Yeah."

What else could he ask? This man had no more answers than Alex. "Did she have any injuries other than the concussion when she had the accident?"

"She had a sprained wrist and had to wear a brace for a few days, but it quickly healed."

Tuck couldn't think of anything else to ask. He concentrated on eating his breakfast. Then he could go see Alex again. A luxury that hadn't been afforded him for four months.

Just as he was ready to clear his dishes, Parker spoke again. "I will tell you this." He paused, and Tuck stared at him, holding his breath. "I'd trust you quicker than I would Lowery. I'm not fond of lawyers, except for Alex. That man reminds me of a snake more than he does a man."

DR. GEORGE GREENFIELD looked up from the file on his desk as his office door opened. The lady entering brought a smile to his lips. Florence Gibbons had been his patient since he'd come to town thirty years ago. They'd both had mates then, and the four of them had shared some fine times.

"Florence, what are you doing here? You told Marybelle you weren't sick."

She settled into the chair across from him before she let her gaze meet his. "No, I'm not sick."

He suspected he knew the reason for her visit. After all, he'd already had Mabel Baxter, Ruth Langford and Edith Hauk in this morning. "If you're here wanting me to encourage Mac to have a baby so you can win that bet, you're wasting your time."

"Who told you about the bet?" she asked guardedly.

"My dear, that bet became known by everyone in town shortly after you agreed to it. But if you must know, I've seen all three of your friends this morning."

"I didn't think they'd be that fast," she muttered, looking away.

George leaned closer, wishing the desk didn't separate them. "Florence, let nature take its course. Be patient."

"I'm afraid of nature," Florence said, and bit down on her full bottom lip.

George was surprised by the interest he felt in that lip. He was too old for such silly thoughts. He cleared his throat. "What does that mean?"

"Doc, I'm wondering if Mac is…is gay!"

Stunned, George stared at Florence before suddenly leaning back in his chair and roaring with laughter.

"It's not funny!" Florence assured him, tears gathering in her eyes.

"Oh, lordy, yes, it is. Don't you remember that talk you asked me to have with Mac when he was fourteen? Jack had already passed away, and you thought it would come better from a man."

"Of course I remember."

"Well, Mac was definitely interested in the ladies then. And I haven't seen any change since he grew up."

"But he won't even date! I've suggested several young ladies and he refuses to even consider spending time with them. I mean, it's not natural, George!"

George reached across the desk to take Florence's hand where it rested on his desk. "Dear heart, I promise you the boy is normal. He's been hurt bad. But I believe time will take care of the problem. You just have to be patient."

"Huh!" Florence responded, her exclamation full of disgust.

ALEX WAS STILL MUNCHING on a muffin when the doorbell rang. Since she was only wearing her night-shirt, she hastened up the stairs for her robe before returning to the front door.

"Hope we're not here too early," Jessica said, holding a wrapped dish.

Melanie, standing just behind her, also carried a covered plate. "We thought we'd bring over some extra things for breakfast."

"How nice of you. Come in. But this really wasn't necessary. Your mother-in-law left milk and muffins."

The two ladies followed her into the condo as she led the way back to the kitchen.

"We know," Melanie said, "but since I've gotten over my morning sickness, I'm always starving at breakfast." She set down her plate and unwrapped it, revealing a fragrant quiche. Jessica's plate held homemade cinnamon rolls.

Alex's mouth watered. "Shouldn't I worry about gaining too much weight?"

"This one time won't hurt. Besides, Doc Green-field doesn't believe in starving yourself when you're pregnant," Jessica assured her. "And if you're going to stay here awhile, you'll be under his care."

"I suppose so." Alex hadn't thought about that aspect of her decision.

"You'll like him," Melanie assured her.

Jessica pulled out paper plates and plastic glasses from a sack she'd carried in and set a carton of milk on the counter. "I'll pour us some milk. Do you need some more, Alex?"

"Yes, please." If she was going to inhale these calories, she'd need more liquid.

Once they were all settled 'round the table, Jessica spoke. "We're not only here to feed our faces. We need to discuss our timetable."

Alex put down the cinnamon roll she'd been eating and stared at the other two women apprehensively. "What timetable?"

"Do you remember last night when I asked you not to tell Mabel about the babies?"

"Yes."

Melanie chimed in. "We haven't told anyone we're pregnant, except our husbands, of course."

"But what does that have to do with me?" Their situations were entirely different from hers.

Jessica and Melanie exchanged conspiratorial smiles. "It's the bet thing," Jessica said.

"I remember you said something about that last night, but I'm not clear about what you meant. Some of the evening is a blur."

"You were tired. And being bombarded with information," Melanie said, smiling at her. "I would've gone down for the count long before you did."

Alex was reminded again of the sense of camaraderie she'd felt last night with these two women. She hadn't found anyone in Dallas like Jessica and Melanie. "You're both so…so kind."

The two exchanged glances that Alex couldn't read. Then Jessica spoke again. "We were going to tell our families about the babies today. We figured at the rate we're growing, they'll figure it out soon anyway."

"But your news threw us into a tailspin," Melanie added.

"Why?"

"Because Tuck's mother is one of the group who made the bet," Melanie explained.

"Explain the bet to me again."

Jessica told her how the four women had made a bet about who would get the first grandchild. "We didn't think any of the guys would marry. We figured that bet had no chance of working. Then Cal and I, well, we finally figured out how each other felt and got married. Two months later, Spence and Melanie followed us down the aisle.

"Then we discovered that we both got pregnant on my wedding day, which meant that each mother has a fifty percent chance of winning. We decided to hold off revealing our pregnancies so that the other mothers would keep trying to marry off their sons."

Melanie continued the story. "We'd just given up and were ready to tell them today, when you arrived last night, pregnant on the same day."

"The stars must've been in the correct alignment," Alex said, a half smile on her face.

"So, we wanted to let you know that we're going to hold off another week or two. Maybe we can have a seventy-five percent rate," Jessica concluded with a smile.

"Or maybe not. I really don't know if this baby is…is Tuck's or not," Alex reminded them. She wished she knew. She wasn't sure what she would do if she knew who the father of her baby was, but the not knowing was difficult.

"Alex," Jessica said, a solemn look on her face, "I didn't know you that long, but I'm a good judge of character. I don't think you would've double-timed Tuck."

"Did I tell you I was sleeping with Tuck?"

"No," Jessica admitted with a sigh. "I mean, we knew something was going on, but not...not how much."

"Tuck has been real down in the dumps the past couple of months," Melanie explained. "We thought he was mooning over you, but he wouldn't ever say. A couple of times, around the time of our wedding, he disappeared for a weekend, never saying where he was going. Afterward, he admitted he'd gone to Dallas."

Alex picked up her cinnamon roll and took a bite, then rose and crossed to the window to stare at the trees budding out. "I'm so confused. I'm sorry, I don't know what to tell you. Even if...if the baby is Tuck's, that doesn't mean I'm going to stay here."

She glanced over her shoulder to see looks mixed of consternation and sympathy.

"You'll just have to give it a little time," Jessica assured her. "I think—"

"Oh, no!" Alex exclaimed, interrupting. "There's a truck pulling in. It's—Tuck. I'm not dressed!" She threw the cinnamon roll back on her plate and ran for the stairs.

WHEN JESSICA OPENED the door to Tuck's impatient knock, he forgot to greet her. "Where's Alex?" he demanded, looking over Jessica's shoulder.

"Good morning to you, too," Jessica said with a smile before answering his question. "She went upstairs to dress."

"Oh. Can I come in?"

"Sure. Where's Bill?"

"He's coming. He stopped off at Cal's office." He followed Jessica into her old condo. As he entered, he sniffed the air. "Cinnamon rolls?"

Jessica chuckled. "Come on. There might be one or two left."

Tuck entered the kitchen and greeted Melanie. Then he checked out what was on the table. "Quiche, too? Hey, I should've gotten here earlier."

Melanie stood and fixed him a plate with both quiche and a cinnamon roll. "I thought real men didn't eat quiche," she teased.

"Tuck never turns down food," Jessica responded.

Tuck ate, ignoring their words.

Until Alex came downstairs.

He rose from his chair, abandoning his second breakfast. "Morning, Alex."

"Good morning, Tuck. I'm sorry I wasn't down—I mean, I overslept this morning."

"Good. You need a lot of rest when you're pregnant," he said, hoping he sounded as though he knew what he was talking about.

"Where's Bill?" she asked, looking around the kitchen anxiously.

"I didn't hurt him," Tuck quickly said. "He wanted to stop and talk to Cal. Said to tell you he'd be here in a few minutes."

"You didn't fight over anything, did you?"

"Nope. I even cooked him breakfast," Tuck assured her, hoping to score some approval points.

Alex stared at the half-filled plate in front of him. "Didn't you eat with him?"

"Yeah, but I can't turn down such good food," Tuck said, smiling at Jessica and Melanie.

"Don't listen to him," Jessica said with a laugh. "This man never turns down food."

"Hey, I work hard," Tuck protested. "It takes a lot of calories to keep me going."

"Both of you should sit down and finish eating," Melanie said, smiling, too. "Tuck, all we have to drink is milk. Do you want some?"

"No, I'd rather have water. I'll get it, though, Mel. You sit down. All of you. I can't believe I'm having breakfast with three pregnant women."

"Uh, Tuck, we're going to keep the babies a secret for a while longer, okay?"

"Why?" he asked, coming back to the table with his glass of water.

"Well, we figured if we waited a few days, maybe your mother would have a chance at winning, too," Jessica said.

Tuck shot a quick look at Alex, noting her red cheeks. "Okay, I won't say anything."

An awkward silence fell over the room. Tuck concentrated on his food, afraid if he spoke he'd upset Alex. He thought he'd scared her last night.

"What was Bill going to ask Cal?" Alex asked.

"I don't know. He didn't say, and I didn't think I should ask." He hoped that response made him sound civil. A reasonable man.

"Maybe we should figure out what you'll need to

live here," Jessica said, ending another awkward silence. "I have some paper in my purse. We'll make a list."

That activity suited Tuck. He wouldn't have to say anything, which left him plenty of time to watch Alex. She was wearing a long denim shirt loose over a pair of jeans. He suspected she'd chosen the shirt to hide her pregnancy.

The sudden urge to run his hands over her body, to discover the changes their child had made, to touch her soft skin, almost caused him to embarrass himself.

"Tuck? Tuck, are you all right?" Jessica said, snapping her fingers in front of his nose.

"Huh? Yeah, what? Did I miss something?"

"I asked if you had any furniture you could contribute to the condo. Mac offered a sofa, that green one of Florence's. Do you have a chair or coffee table to go with it?"

"Please, that isn't necessary," Alex protested. "I won't be entertaining or anything."

Tuck loved the way her cheeks reddened, making her look like an embarrassed child. He wanted to cuddle her in his lap, assure her that he'd protect her and their baby.

"Tuck! You're not paying attention," Jessica protested, and he turned to stare at her, frowning.

"I think he has other things on his mind," Melanie said, grinning.

"What are you talking about?" Tuck demanded. Somehow he'd lost track of the conversation.

"Never mind. We'll come out to your ranch and

raid it. You probably won't even notice anything is gone," Jessica said.

A knock on the door prevented Tuck from answering. Alex and Jessica both rose to answer it. Jessica laughed and sat back down. "I forgot. It's your place now."

Alex returned almost immediately with Bill Parker following her. "Bill, you remember Jessica and Melanie from last night?"

"Of course. Good morning, ladies."

"Would you care for a cinnamon roll or a slice of quiche?" Melanie asked.

"No, I had a fine breakfast at Tuck's," Bill replied, raising an eyebrow at Tuck's half-empty plate.

"Did you talk to Cal?" Alex asked.

"Yeah. He confirmed the dates of your visits." Bill turned and looked at Tuck though he spoke to Alex. "He couldn't confirm that you'd had relations with Tuck. They all realized there was an attraction between the two of you, but Tuck hadn't told them anything."

Tuck stiffened. "It's ill-mannered to kiss and tell."

Bill shrugged.

"Didn't you tell anyone?" Alex asked.

"Did you? You were there too, you know," he pointed out, failing to hide his irritation.

Alex dropped her gaze. "No. No, I didn't."

He felt as if he'd kicked a puppy. "Alex, what we had…it happened so quickly. Then you went away and told me not to come visit you. You didn't answer my calls." He cleared his throat. "It was almost as if it hadn't happened."

He wasn't sure she would've responded, but before she could, someone else knocked at the door.

This time Alex led Cal into the kitchen. He immediately gave Jessica a kiss. Then, before he could be offered any breakfast, he spoke.

"Just had a call at my office. Someone's looking for you, Alex."

"Me? Who could be calling? My office? Did they—"

"It was Chad Lowery."

Chapter Four

Alex's nerves tightened into a knot that made it hard to swallow. And told her how good the visit to Cactus, Texas, had been for her.

"Why would he call you?" Tuck asked Cal, anger in his voice.

Cal grinned. "Because we're such a small place he figured the sheriff would know if any strangers were in town."

General laughter from these people she now considered her friends helped ease her tension. A little. Until Tuck whirled around to glare at her.

"Are you going to call him? And why does he think he has the right to keep track of you? Didn't you tell him he's not the father?"

All those questions and no answers. These days, she never had answers. As frustrated as Tuck seem to be, she snapped. "I don't know, I don't know, and no." Then she leapt to her feet and paced over to the window, staring out as she had earlier, her arms crossed under her breasts.

Jessica spoke in the awkward silence that followed. "Tuck, you keep forgetting Alex has lost her memory."

A gusty sigh drew Alex's gaze. Tuck didn't exactly look repentant, but his anger seemed to have gone away. In a calmer voice, he repeated one of his questions. "Are you going to call him?"

Alex lifted her chin, prepared for more anger. "I suppose so. It could be work-related."

Even Bill Parker wasn't buying that answer. But though he shook his head, he also dug into his jacket pocket, pulled out his cell phone and held it out to her.

Without saying anything, Cal handed her a piece of paper where he'd written down the number Chad had left.

Tuck stared at her, as if he expected her to make the phone call while he stood beside her. No way. Two difficult men at once was more than she could handle. "I'll go upstairs, if you don't mind. I'm sure I won't be long."

She hurried up the stairs in full retreat.

TUCK HADN'T WANTED HER to call the jerk privately. But he could understand why she did. But he still didn't like it. He turned back to Cal. "What did the man say?"

"He was trying to locate Alexandra Logan, an attorney from Dallas who had represented Jessica Hoya." Cal shrugged his shoulders. "When I told him she was here, he asked me to have her call him, that's all."

Tuck didn't bother with the niceties of polite conversation. With a nod to his friend, he looked at Bill Parker. "She didn't tell him she was coming here?"

"You'll have to ask Alex," Bill said calmly, relaxed in his chair. "I may be her investigator, but I'm not her keeper."

Jessica leaned forward. "What is this man like? Have you met him?"

"Yes," Bill responded, his gaze going to Tuck.

Tuck guessed Bill was wondering if he'd repeat Bill's assessment of Lowery, and he barely shook his head to reassure him. He wasn't going to say anything about that, but he liked Bill's words. They comforted him.

"Is he...is he a nice man?" Melanie asked.

"Well, now, Mrs. Hauk, he's...respectable. But I don't know that he's telling the truth."

"Of course he's not," Cal replied, his voice steady.

"How do you know?" Jessica quickly demanded.

"Because if he is, Tuck's a liar and Alex is a...loose woman," he said, apparently choosing those words as a last minute substitute. "I find those two things to be unacceptable."

"Thanks," Tuck muttered, a wry grin on his face.

"Of course not," Jessica said staunchly, "but... but things happen. I know Tuck *thinks* he's the daddy, I mean, I'm *sure* he— I want him to be the daddy. But accidents happen."

"No!" Tuck protested. He didn't even want to consider such a thing.

Before the discussion could continue, Alex returned to the kitchen. It was obvious to everyone that she was upset, even as she tried to muster a smile when she handed the phone back to Bill with her thanks.

Anger filled Tuck again, but he was determined not to add to her stress. Unless he had to. Standing, he rounded the table, ignoring Alex's flinch as he came near. He pulled out her chair and then urged her into it, his fingers going to her shoulders and neck as she sat.

"Tuck—" she began in protest.

He shushed her and began massaging the coiled tension in her shoulders. "Just relax, Alex. All this stress isn't good for the baby. Or you."

His reward came when she leaned her head against him, her shoulders slumping. That, of course, was in addition to his getting to touch her, to feel her silken skin again.

Bill stared at Tuck, as if assessing his intent. Apparently satisfied, he looked at Alex. "Is everything all right?"

"Yes, of course. Chad was being his obnoxious self, demanding that I return to Dallas, enraged that I hadn't sought his approval for my plans."

She let her eyes close and Tuck fought to keep his own tension level under control.

"Are you two engaged?" Cal asked, referring to Alex and Chad.

Tuck almost left a bruise on Alex's shoulder at his friend's question. He fought for control as he waited for Alex's answer.

"No! He said— We agreed— I won't make any commitments until I get my memory back."

It was not the answer Tuck wanted to hear. He wanted Alex to assure their audience that she believed Tuck. That the baby was his. That Chad Lowery had no hold over her life. That she remembered how magical they had been together.

"Did you tell him you were going to stay here for a while?" Jessica asked.

Alex shook her head no. "I told him I would let him know as soon as I recovered my memory, or...or something else happened to clarify my difficulties. That's all."

Tuck released his pent-up breath and resumed the massage that had halted as he'd waited for her response.

"Mr. Parker, are you going back to Dallas today?" Melanie asked.

The investigator smiled at her. "Those were my plans, as long as Alex doesn't need me here. You all seem willing to lend her some support, and I think she needs to stop thinking about everything so much. What do you think, Alex? Will you be okay without me?"

"Yes, Bill," she agreed with a nod. "I think a few weeks spent in Cactus may help me, as you suggested. And you're only a phone call away."

Jessica snapped her fingers. "If you had a phone! I hadn't thought of that. We'll need to get the phone service restored. I'll pay for it," she hurriedly added.

"That's okay, Jessica. I don't have money problems."

"Actually," Bill said, "when you go back to Dallas to pack a few things, you can get *your* cell phone." He looked at the others. "She didn't bring it with her because she wasn't expecting calls and I had mine with me."

"That's true, but if you're going back today, when—"

"I'll take you after you've rested up," Tuck hastily offered. He wasn't about to give up the opportunity to be in a car with Alex for seven hours twice. They could do a lot of talking in that time.

"I hate to take that much of your time," she said stiffly, and he could feel her tensing up again.

"No problem. I've made the trip several times lately. I know the road well." He didn't add that he'd driven it to find her, but everyone knew.

"If that's settled," Bill Parker said, standing, "then I'll be on my way. I've got several cases hanging that need my attention. Alex, call me when you get to Dallas. I'll keep checking on...things. And take care of yourself."

Alex got up from her chair, dislodging Tuck's hands. He felt an immediate loss that shook him with its intensity, but he couldn't complain.

She moved into Bill's embrace, thanking him for his assistance. Then the others shook his hand and wished him a good trip. Tuck was the last to speak to him.

"I'll take care of her," he promised in a low voice.

"I know you will. Just be careful about pressuring her," Bill warned quietly, but he was smiling.

Tuck nodded. Then the man was gone, leaving silence in the room.

"Nice guy," Cal commented finally.

Alex wrapped her arms around herself. Tuck had to forcibly restrain his arms from seconding hers.

"Yes, he's been wonderful. I—I sometimes felt

like I'd lost my mind before I found him.'' She gave a bitter laugh. ''Maybe I have.''

Tuck didn't bother with any restraint then. He wrapped his arms around Alex and held her against him. To his surprise and pleasure, she turned around and buried her face against his neck. Unfortunately, he attributed her response to Bill's leaving rather than to him.

''I have an idea,'' he said over Alex's shoulder. ''Why don't I take Alex out to my place for a tour and a leisurely lunch while you put together what she'll need here.''

He was asking a lot of his friends, but he knew they'd agree. He and the guys had been friends forever, and Jessica and Melanie fit right in. They all relied on each other.

''That's a good idea,'' Jessica immediately responded. ''Then you can bring her back here for an afternoon nap, and we'll all meet for dinner at the Roundup.''

''She might be tired of a crowd at every meal,'' Tuck suggested. He had a more intimate dinner in mind.

Alex, proving she was listening to the discussion, pushed out of his arms. ''No, I enjoyed being with everyone last night.''

As if they'd all read his mind, his friends were staring at him, warning in their gazes. Cal became the spokesman. ''She'll have plenty of time for quiet nights, Tuck. After all, she's staying for a while.''

Back off. You're pushing too hard.

Okay, okay, he could take a hint. But he didn't like it. He nodded. ''You'd better get a jacket before we go, Alex. It's spring, but there's a brisk breeze out there.''

She nodded and hurried up the stairs.

Jessica spoke as soon as Alex was out of the kitchen. "Tuck, don't— I mean, I know the two of you will be alone, but she's not ready—''

"I'm not going to seduce her, Jess. I'm not an idiot," he snapped, hoping no one realized that the possibility had caused his pulse to race. "I'm going to show her the animals, let her think about something other than the mess her life is in. Help her relax.''

"Good for you," Melanie said, leaning over to kiss his cheek. Jessica did the same, squeezing his arm.

"We'll see you at the restaurant about seven?" Cal suggested. "I'll call Mac, and Mel will tell Spence. We'll swing by here and pick up Alex.''

Tuck wanted to protest that he would pick up Alex, but Cal was right. Pressing her right now would be the wrong thing to do. "Agreed," he said with a sigh.

"THE BABY CALVES are so darling," Alex exclaimed, the most relaxed smile he'd yet seen on her lips. "They're sparkling clean and they bounce when they trot around.''

"Yeah. You're seeing them at the best time. In a few months, they'll be a lot heavier. And dirtier. Spring is special out here.''

She took a deep breath and turned her smile on him. He thought he'd melt right there. The Alex of old—bold, confident, irresistibly sexy—was beside him.

"What's it like in the other seasons?" she asked.

He didn't remind her that she'd seen it in the fall. He'd worked hard to keep her day stress-free. "Well, in winter, you wouldn't have that window rolled down. We don't have heavy snowfall, but it gets cold and the icy wind cuts right through you."

She shivered, easing back from the pickup window as if she felt that wind.

"Then, in summer, things heat up out here. It stays kind of cool at night, but that sun gets mean during the day. By the summer's end, everything's turned brown. Just when you think you can't stand it anymore, fall comes in with a blast, bringing a little rain, if we're lucky, and cooler temperatures."

"Sounds dramatic."

"It can be. We sometimes have cookouts in the fall, when a fire feels good." He watched her out of the corner of his eye, wondering if she'd have any memories of the celebration they'd had at his ranch for Jessica.

She only smiled.

"Then, just when you're settling in for winter, Indian summer comes along."

"It gets hot again?"

"Well, warm, at least."

She smiled again and stared at the cows. "Where are the horses? You do have horses, don't you?"

"Sure. They're in a pasture next to the barns." Without saying anything else, he slipped the truck into gear and drove slowly over the pasture toward the house. He normally bounced along at a higher speed, always impatient, but he didn't think that rough a ride would be good for a pregnant woman.

After she petted several of the horses, showing no recognition when he offered the names of the ones she'd petted before, they returned to the house. He'd bypassed it earlier.

"Uh-oh," he muttered without thinking as he noted his mother's car. He'd called her and asked her to bring out lunch, but he'd hoped she'd leave it and return home before he and Alex made it to the house.

Instead, she was waiting.

"What's wrong?"

"Nothing. Mom's here with our lunch."

"Really? It's awfully nice of her to go to so much trouble. You didn't have to feed me."

"Mom likes to cook." True, but her interest today would be in Alex, not the meal. "Uh, don't forget, we're not going to mention any of the pregnancies, okay?"

"I remember."

He parked the truck and got out to come around and help her down. It was a great excuse to touch her. But she was already on the ground.

"You should've let me help you," he muttered, taking her arm to lead her to the house.

"I can manage. It's my head that's messed up, not my legs."

His gaze traveled over her long legs, remembering the smooth skin, the strength of those legs as they'd wrapped around him, holding him close. He sucked in a deep breath and tried to dismiss those images.

Maybe it *was* a good thing that his mother was here.

ALEX BREATHED EASIER as they approached the house.

The man beside her was so attractive, she had to constantly fight her response to him. The touch of his hand had her blood pressure climbing. She was glad they wouldn't be alone for lunch.

The attraction she felt gave her a new piece of information, however. There had been something between them. She didn't know exactly what, or how intense it was, but the tension she felt in his presence was different from her feelings about everyone else in Cactus.

It made his claim a real possibility.

As they approached the back porch, the door opened and a tall, attractive woman smiled at her.

"Alex," she exclaimed, reaching out to hug Alex when she came closer. "It's so good to see you again."

"Thank you, Mrs. Langford," she said, smiling.

"Mom, Alex has lost her memory," Tuck hurriedly said, making Alex feel like the star attraction at a freak show.

His mother ignored him and urged Alex into the house. "You come right in. It may be spring, but that wind still has some teeth."

Alex smiled again, enjoying the warmth in the lady's voice. Her own mother had died of cancer when she was seventeen. She missed the nurturing that a mother never stops giving her children, whether it's wanted or not.

"Sit right down at the table. I've got some hot soup to start you off. It'll take off the chill."

"Mom," Tuck protested. "It's seventy degrees outside, not twenty. And we can serve ourselves."

Alex could tell by his mother's reaction, quickly hidden, that she was hurt by her son's dismissal. Even if she hadn't wanted the woman to stay for her own reasons, she would've invited her for that one.

"I'd love for you to join us, Mrs. Langford. I have so many questions about Cactus, Tuck will probably be glad of some assistance. Won't you, Tuck?" She warned him with her gaze that she'd accept no less than his agreement.

"Sure, Mom, if there's enough food."

The bum! He was showing her an escape hatch, so she could gracefully turn down Alex's invitation. Alex smiled at Mrs. Langford. "Don't worry. I don't eat that much these days. I'm sure there'll be plenty."

"Well, if you're sure, I'd enjoy a chance to visit with you," she agreed. "And please, call me Ruth. We're not formal out here."

"Thank you, Ruth. May I wash my hands at the sink?" Alex asked. She didn't dare excuse herself to a bathroom. She knew if she did Ruth would be gone when she returned to the kitchen.

Tuck tried. He suggested she go to the hall bathroom. She politely declined, turning on the water at the sink. He frowned and then stalked out of the room.

"Maybe I should go. Tuck seems—"

"I'd really like you to stay. Tuck can get a lit-

tle…intense, and I'm supposed to relax.'' She tried
to look vulnerable, to underline her words. It was a
role she didn't have much difficulty playing lately.

"Oh, you poor dear. Of course, I'll stay. He's
always been that way, you know. Frank, my husband, says it's good. He says that means Tuck will
succeed in life because he knows what he wants and
goes after it.'' She looked over her shoulder guiltily.
"I don't mean— He's a wonderful boy.''

"Yes, he is,'' Alex agreed with a smile. Already
she knew that about Tuck, even without her memory. She couldn't believe he was single. What was
wrong with the women in Cactus? "I'm surprised
he's not married.''

"Me, too,'' Ruth said, looking down in the
mouth. "I mean, I've encouraged him to find a wife.
A rancher needs one. Look at this kitchen. He's got
the money to redo the house, but he says there's
nothing wrong with it.''

Well, here, at least, was one thing she could reassure Ruth Langford about. "I think he's planning
on making some changes. He asked me if I'd help
him pick out wallpaper and a stove and things.''

"Really?'' Ruth asked in surprise. "When did he
say that?''

"Last night. I'm going to stay in Cactus for a few
weeks, to recuperate. I can't work until my memory
returns, and they, Tuck and his friends, offered me
a place to stay, and things to occupy my mind.''

"That's terrific. You fit in so well around here,
and I'm sure Tuck will enjoy your company.'' As
if realizing she might have overstepped the mark,
she said, "I mean, you being friends and all.''

Embarrassed, Alex sought a change in subject. "Yes, and maybe he'll go ahead and update his kitchen."

"Cleaning it would help," Ruth drawled, grinning as she looked around her. "I was embarrassed to serve you food in here."

"It's not that bad," Alex said, but she laughed. It felt good to feel her sense of humor emerge. "I'm not that much better at cleaning my own kitchen when I've put in twelve hours at the office."

"Tuck could afford a housekeeper, but he said he didn't want anyone else in his house." Ruth shook her head in disgust.

"Maybe he'll change his mind once the kitchen looks different."

They heard Tuck approaching. Ruth turned toward the door, smiling at her son as he came into the kitchen. "I'm glad to hear there are going to be some changes around here in four or five months," she said as a greeting.

He came to a dead stop and whipped his gaze to Alex's face, his cheeks paling. "You told her?"

Chapter Five

"Was it going to be a surprise?" Ruth asked, staring at him.

Tuck didn't know what to say. His mother was certainly taking the news about the baby very calmly. Fortunately, before he could say the wrong thing, Alex spoke.

"Sorry, Tuck. I didn't know you hadn't told your mother about *redoing the kitchen*." There was a twinkle in her eye he hadn't seen since her return.

"The...the kitchen. Right. I was going to, uh, surprise Mom, but I should've reminded you." He shrugged his shoulders as he turned to his mother, hoping to convince her it was the kitchen that he was talking about. "What do you think, Mom? I asked Alex to help me make decisions."

"I can't think of anyone better," Ruth assured him, almost gloating.

Uh-oh. He saw the matchmaking wheels engage. His normal response to his mother's attempts to marry him off was a need to run for the hills. Then he froze. He *wanted* to marry Alex. Not only

wanted, he *intended* to marry Alex. He and his mom
were on the same side, for once.

He smiled. "Me, neither."

Both women stared at him, as if he'd said something bizarre, but he ignored them, and settled in his
chair at the table. "The soup smells good, Mom."

Ruth shook herself out of her trance and filled
their bowls. She joined them at the table and, between bites, launched into a discussion of the
kitchen project.

AFTER A LONG AFTERNOON nap, Alex prepared for
dinner at The Last Roundup. She was amazed at the
difference a little more than twenty-four hours made.
For the past month she'd scarcely been interested in
food, and sleep had come in small chunks.

Today at lunch, with Ruth's company, as well as
Tuck's, she'd eaten a good lunch and enjoyed herself. Planning the kitchen was fun, especially since
Tuck agreed to anything the two women had suggested.

Alex sighed. Even though she'd discovered her
life had centered around work, somehow she
thought her interests had changed. Maybe she'd
grown tired of working long hours, of the lack of
variety in her life.

Her choice of clothing for the evening was limited, she decided as she looked in her suitcase. In
fact, she'd need to go to Dallas tomorrow to replen-
ish her wardrobe. Tonight, she slipped into a navy
suit with a soft cream sweater under the jacket. More
business than social, but it seemed her wardrobe resembled her life.

When she joined Cal and Jessica, her friend commented on how well rested she appeared.

"That's because I slept all afternoon."

"Ah. See, we were right about your staying here," Jessica said with a smile.

"Yes, you were, and I can't tell you how much I appreciate the offer. We didn't discuss rent, but I'll be glad to pay—"

"Absolutely not."

They drove the short distance to the restaurant and joined the rest of their friends. Alex ended up sitting next to Tuck, at his insistence, but she felt safe surrounded by the others.

Not that he threatened her or made her do anything she didn't want to do. No, she was the problem. Already, she found herself hanging on his every word, craving one of his sexy smiles, his touch.

Chad Lowery never affected her this way.

She gave a special thanks that Tuck had worked so hard to get in touch with her. She'd been so confused and upset when she'd realized she didn't remember anything. The doctor had informed her of her pregnancy in the hospital in Washington. Chad had told her the baby was his.

But something didn't seem right. Only there didn't seem to be any other candidates. When she hired Bill Parker, and he went over her credit card bills and talked to her secretary, he'd wanted to know about Cactus, Texas. And Tuck Langford.

Tuck slid his arm around the back of her chair even as he leaned forward to argue with Cal about a horse he wanted to buy. She sank back in the chair, practically sitting in his embrace, drawing in the scent of man and leather, and a hint of spice.

She hadn't been sure he'd speak to her this evening, because after lunch she'd ridden back to town with Ruth. A look in his eye told her he'd wanted a goodbye kiss.

So had she.

But that wasn't wise. She needed to recover her memory. If the baby turned out to be Chad's, she'd have to decide what she was going to do about him. And about Tuck. She wasn't sure he'd be interested in another man's baby.

He leaned closer and placed his lips near her ear. "You okay?"

"Yes, of course," she hurriedly replied, afraid her dismal thoughts had shown on her face. When he kissed her cheek before returning to the conversation, shivers coursed through her. Her gaze met Jessica's and they exchanged smiles.

Mac leaned toward her. "When are you coming to visit my office?"

"I don't know. I need to go back to Dallas soon to get more clothes, or I'll be wandering around town naked," she joked, smiling at him.

Tuck replied rather than Mac. "We can't have that. It'd cause a stampede."

Cal chuckled. "More than that, it'd cause a fight. Because I guarantee you'd be fighting every man in town."

"I was joking," Alex hurriedly said, her cheeks turning red.

"We know," Tuck agreed. "But it's an interesting thought." He waggled his eyebrows. "Do you feel up to the trip to Dallas tomorrow?"

"Tomorrow?" she asked, surprised. "Yes, of course, but can you spare the time? I know you have a lot of work to do."

"I'll manage. If we leave about seven in the morning, you'll have some of the afternoon left when we arrive. We can spend the night and come back the next day. Will that give you enough time?"

"Yes, thank you. More than enough. I won't have to go to the office or…or anything. Just pack some clothes, arrange to have my mail forwarded. Things like that."

His fingers were stroking her far shoulder, and she could scarcely think. The urge to fall against him, let her head rest on his shoulder, was almost overpowering.

"Will you trust me enough to let me sleep on your couch? Or should I get a hotel room?"

Her gaze leapt to his face. Trust him? She thought she trusted him. She wasn't sure she trusted herself. "I—I suppose you can sleep on the couch, but it won't be all that comfortable."

She suddenly realized everyone at the table was listening to their conversation. Would they think her rude after all they'd offered her?

"Tuck," Jessica said softly.

"Yeah?" he replied, but he continued to stare at Alex.

"A hotel room would be a good idea."

He jerked his head toward Jessica, but Alex could see the frown on his face.

"Really, Jessica," Alex hurriedly said, "if he wants to sleep on the couch, I don't mind."

Mac added, "It's the no-stress thing, Tuck. We promised Bill."

"So my life is now decided by group vote?" he growled, scowling at his friend.

Melanie chuckled. "I thought that was the way you guys have always made decisions."

Spence grinned. "Not about the ladies. You'll notice Tuck didn't asked our opinion before he fathered Alex's baby."

"Neither did you," his wife reminded him.

"Yeah. The only one who's stayed out of trouble is Mac," Spence said.

"And I'm going to keep it that way," Mac assured him firmly even as he smiled. Then he changed the subject. "I hear the band playing tonight is really good."

"Yes," Jessica said. "Anyone want to go in and hear them, maybe dance a little?"

After her nap earlier today, Alex didn't feel she could plead tiredness. Besides, listening to a live band sounded like fun. It was the dancing that had her worried.

TUCK STOOD and waited for Alex to precede him. But he didn't follow her at once. Instead, he grabbed Jessica's arm.

"Jess, I wasn't going to pull anything. But I think someone should stay with her. Lowery might find out she's there, try to persuade her to stay." His voice was a raw whisper, filled with worry. He couldn't deny his concern.

"Oh. I hadn't thought of that," Jessica muttered.

"What's up?" Cal asked, having realized his wife wasn't at his side and come back for her.

Instead of answering his question, Jessica looked at Tuck. "I know. Melanie and I will go with you. We'll stay at Alex's condo and you can go to a hotel."

That wasn't the answer Tuck wanted. He'd looked forward to time alone with Alex.

"Wait a minute. You don't need a seven-hour ride. It won't be good for the baby," Cal whispered hoarsely, glaring at Tuck even as he spoke to his wife.

"You thought it would be all right for Alex. She's just as pregnant as I am. And Melanie, too."

"But I don't want you to go away for the night," Cal complained.

Tuck didn't want to take Jessica and Melanie, but he couldn't keep from grinning at his friend. "I think you're whining, Cal."

Cal glared at him. "Just 'cause you don't have a woman doesn't mean I should be deprived of mine!"

Tuck glared right back. "I've got a woman. I just have to convince her."

"You two stop arguing. Being apart one night will make you appreciate me more, Cal. Now come on before someone notices we're not there." Jessica hurried to catch up with their friends.

"Thanks, Tuck," Cal said, not sounding grateful at all.

"Hey, I'm not any happier about this than you are."

"Maybe Spence will come up with a reason Melanie can't go. Let's go talk to him."

"That won't keep Jess from going and you know it. She's as hardheaded as you," Tuck reminded him.

"Yeah, I know."

They entered the dance hall portion of the restaurant, having to wait at the door for their eyes to adjust to the darkness.

"There they are," Cal finally said, pointing to their left as he headed in that direction.

When the pair of them arrived at the large table Jessica had commandeered for them, they grabbed Spence and walked a few feet away to inform him of Jessica's decision.

Spence determined he'd just tell Melanie she couldn't go. Cal and Tuck exchanged a look. They didn't know Melanie as well as they did Jessica, but they suspected Spence's solution didn't have a chance.

Suddenly, Tuck didn't care what Jessica and Melanie did. His focus was on the dance floor where Alex was in the arms of a cowboy, two-stepping around the room.

Without a word to his friends, he strode onto the floor and tapped the stranger on the shoulder. "I'm cutting in," he announced.

The man stepped back in surprise and Tuck didn't hesitate. Wrapping an arm around Alex, he waltzed her across the floor.

"Tuck! That was rude."

He ignored her words. "What are you doing

dancing with a stranger? He could be a mass murderer, for all you know!''

''Mac knows him,'' Alex assured him, looking down her perfect little nose at him, even though she had to look up.

''I don't care who knows him. You should be dancing with me.'' He pulled her a little bit closer and dropped her hand to wrap both arms around her. He laid his face against her silky hair and breathed in its flowery scent.

Her hands rested on his chest, her arms working as barriers to her body. ''Put your hands around my neck,'' he whispered.

After a brief hesitation, she did as he asked and he pulled her even closer, feeling her softness from his head to his toes. And loving every second of it.

''Tuck,'' she whispered, ''We're not moving much.''

''It's a slow dance.''

''Not this slow,'' she assured him.

Afraid she'd pull back, he moved his feet a little more. Hell, he'd dance a jig, as long as she let him hold her, something he'd been longing to do since she'd walked into the restaurant last night.

Or since she'd last left Cactus.

He might be mad at her. He might wonder why she didn't tell him she was pregnant when she found out. He might even question her relationship with Chad Lowery.

But he never stopped wanting her. And never would.

''Tuck, the music's stopped,'' Alex whispered.

''Huh? Oh. Oh, well, you want to sit down?''

"Yes," she said, a hint of apology in her voice. "I'm feeling a little tired."

With one arm wrapped around her in support, he walked her back to the table, only to discover an argument in progress.

"You don't trust me to go away for one night? With one of your friends?" Melanie asked, her voice rising.

"It's not that I don't trust you, honey." Spence was trying to sound reasonable but not succeeding. "It's that it is an unnecessary risk."

"So is chasing those stupid cows, but I don't stop you from doing it."

"Chasing—" Spence began, stunned, then stopped to swallow and try again. "Now, honey, you're not being reasonable. You know that's my job. I didn't argue with you about your business."

"What's going on?" Alex asked, a worried look on her face.

"Nothing," Jessica and Melanie both said at the same time.

Tuck pulled out a chair for Alex, then sat beside her. "These two ladies want to go with us to Dallas. Their husbands don't want them to."

"Go with us?" Alex asked, staring at Tuck. "But why?"

Before Tuck could say anything, if he had an answer, Jessica said, "I haven't been to Dallas in a while. I thought maybe we could do a little shopping while we're there."

"There wouldn't be time unless we stayed an extra day," Alex said consideringly. "I don't know if Tuck could stay away that long."

"We don't even need Tuck," Melanie said, with a determined look at her husband. "I can drive us in my Lexus."

Spence and Cal both shouted, "No!"

Tuck took it a step further. "I'm going with Alex, whether you two come or not. I'm borrowing my mother's Cadillac, so you'll all be comfortable, and I'm willing to stay as long as you want. But I'll be there."

"Please, I don't want to cause any problems," Alex protested. "I can rent a car, or...or catch a flight from Lubbock—"

"Nope," Tuck replied. "I'm going with you."

"And we are, too," Jessica insisted. "If there were a conference on ranch management, or law enforcement, these two wouldn't hesitate to kiss us goodbye and be out the door. We reserve the same right."

"She's got you there," Mac said, smiling at Spence and Cal.

Cal gave him a disgusted look. "You'd better hope you never connect up with a lady, Mac, 'cause if you do, we're gonna have a payback. It's no fair siding with the ladies."

"I'm not siding with the ladies. I only pointed out that Jessica had a good point." Mac's smile turned a little grim. "But I don't have to worry because I'm not marrying again."

None of the men had a response. After all, Tuck reminded himself, it wasn't the first time Mac had expressed his feelings.

Jessica, however, said, "Don't be too sure.

You're not the only one who said that. And look at what's happened."

"Fifty percent success, I know," Mac returned. "But not a hundred percent."

"Maybe seventy-five percent," Melanie added, shifting her gaze to Tuck and Alex before bringing it back to Mac.

Mac shrugged his shoulders. "You've got enough to argue about without worrying about my future."

Which, of course, reminded Spence and Cal of their problem.

"Wait a minute," Cal said, "when we started this argument we were talking about one day away. Now you want two days?"

"Serves you right," Jessica returned. "I wouldn't have thought about shopping if you hadn't fussed at me."

"But you said that was why you were going," Alex said, a frown on her face. "Why were you going originally?"

Tuck grimaced as he waited for Jessica to come up with an explanation that didn't involve Chad Lowery. He hoped she came up with one.

"To keep you company," Jessica said, smiling. "But then I thought a little shopping would be a good idea. And it'll keep us from getting so tired."

"Okay," Tuck said, as if everything was settled. "I want to leave at seven in the morning. So maybe we'd better cut the evening short. I haven't packed." He stood and held out a hand for Alex.

She put her hand in his, which pleased him as his fingers curled around hers, but she didn't stand. "Is that okay with all of you?"

"It's perfect," Melanie assured her, standing.

"Me, too," Jessica agreed. "I like to get an early start. I'll fix a thermos of coffee and bring some juice."

"I'll get Maria to make some cinnamon rolls," Melanie added.

Alex stood, her gaze going to Cal and Spence, looking for confirmation of their wives' cheerfulness. With obvious reluctance, both men nodded.

"Then I'll see you in the morning," Alex said.

Tuck didn't wait for any more conversation. He led her out of the restaurant to his truck.

After he'd started the truck and backed out of the parking lot, she asked, "Do you think they're all okay with everything?"

He laughed. "Probably not. Cal and Spence don't take kindly to their ladies leaving home. But Jess and Mel are hardheaded. No one could stop them from going now."

"But I don't understand why they're so insistent."

Tuck felt guilty. Finally, with a sigh, he admitted, "It's my fault."

"Why?"

"The reason I asked about sleeping on your couch is because I didn't want to leave you alone in case Lowery found out you were in town."

"He may be obnoxious, Tuck, but he wouldn't hurt me."

"But I bet he'd up your stress level again."

"*You* do that, but I don't see you keeping your distance."

"Hey! I've tried to go easy on you." He felt hurt at her words.

She smiled. "I know you have. But…but there's something between us. Something different from the others."

"I would think so. We've made a baby, Alex. We've shared the ultimate intimacy. And," he paused dramatically, "unlike the others, I'm going to kiss you good night."

Chapter Six

Alex hoped Tuck wouldn't pick her up first this morning. She didn't think it would be a good idea to be alone with him after last night.

He hadn't been lying. He'd kissed her good night. And good morning. *Hello. How are you. I'd like to have sex with you.* All those messages had been conveyed in a most delightful fashion.

In fact, if Tuck hadn't pulled back, she might have agreed to anything he asked. Amazing. She hadn't thought she'd been a weak woman, but when Tuck touched her, she went all to pieces.

Did Chad Lowery affect her the same way?

She didn't think so. He had stirred nothing in her when she'd been around him the past month. Panic filled her at the thought that he might be the father of her baby, but not the man she wanted.

The sound of a car had her racing to the front window in time to see Tuck emerge from a brand-new Cadillac. No one else was in the car.

Steeling herself to be friendly but distant, she hurried to the front door. Her suitcase was waiting beside it, ready to go.

"Morning, Tuck," she said as she opened the front door and bent to pick up her suitcase.

Tuck didn't waste time on words. He took her shoulders, pulling her upright before she could grab her bag, and his lips descended to hers.

Several minutes later he offered her a husky good morning.

She could barely think, much less speak. Resting her forehead on his shoulder, she whispered, "I don't think we'd better—I mean, I can't think when— Good morning," she echoed finally, giving up the effort.

He hugged her as he chuckled. Then he released her, picked up her bag and, with an arm around her, led the way to the car. "Give me your keys and I'll lock up."

She handed them over and slid into the front seat. "Oh! I wondered if you'd mind if I brought a pillow. I—I sometimes take naps."

"No problem. I'll get one for you."

She leaned back in the seat, feeling pampered, protected and loved. Loved? That word had her stiffening her spine. She didn't mean loved. Tuck had never mentioned love. She felt—wanted. Yes, that was what he'd shown her. That he wanted her.

Which was pretty remarkable considering she was four months pregnant.

But the most remarkable thing about her time in Cactus was how relaxed, how happy, she'd felt, even without her memory. In Dallas, she'd seemed to stay in a constant state of anxiety.

And she was returning to Dallas.

Panic began to build in her. Was she making a

mistake? Should she stay here, buy new clothes, and ignore her life there? What was so frightening in Dallas?

Tuck returned to the car, both a pillow and a light blanket under his arm. He slid behind the wheel and handed the items to her, a smile on his face.

"Tuck, I think this is a bad idea," she said abruptly.

"We'll put them in the trunk if you don't want them now," he said, misunderstanding her words.

"No. I mean, going to Dallas. I'll—I'll buy some clothes. There's no need to drive all the way back for something to wear." She couldn't believe her voice was shaking.

Tuck slid a warm hand around her neck, his thumb lifting her chin so she'd look at him. "Sweetheart, what's wrong?"

"I don't know. I just don't want to go back."

He leaned over and caressed her lips briefly. Not the soul-searing kisses of a few minutes ago, but a touch filled with warmth and caring. "I'm not going to leave you there, no matter what happens. And you won't be alone. The girls are going with us, remember?"

She couldn't protest any more. She'd look foolish to cancel everything now. And there was nothing to be afraid of. She was being silly.

"Of course. Sorry. Last-minute nerves, I guess." She clutched the pillow and blanket to her and stared straight ahead.

Tuck stroked her cheek, and she wasn't sure she'd convinced him until he released her and started the car.

As they headed for Cal's ranch, a delicious aroma penetrated Alex's fog. "What's that smell?"

Tuck grinned at her. "Mom made us breakfast. She fixed her sausage rolls and had them ready when I picked up the car this morning."

"Mmm, I can't wait. We're going to have enough breakfast to last us halfway to Dallas."

"And then we'll stop for lunch." He smiled.

She smiled back. "You're in an awfully good mood."

"Sweetheart, my mood has been getting better and better ever since you came back to town. Ask anyone. I was surly as a goat until then."

She took a deep breath. Statements such as that made her weak in the knees. "I remember that first night," she finally said. "Though you didn't act too happy to see me."

He sent her a brief glance before turning his attention back to the road. "I was angry."

"Because I hadn't called you?"

"Yeah."

"But you weren't angry anymore once you knew I'd lost my memory."

He took too long to answer.

"Tuck?"

The teasing, the pretense that all was well, went right out the window. "I don't think this is a good time to discuss the past."

"You're still angry?" Her blood pressure shot up. She hadn't realized how much it would hurt not to have Tuck in her corner.

"Not angry, exactly. I—I have some questions."

"About what?"

His fingers tightened on the wheel. "Like why you didn't let me know when you found out you were pregnant."

"I had amnesia."

"You knew you were pregnant before the accident. Bill Parker said you'd already seen a doctor in Dallas."

She'd forgotten that.

"And I'd like to know why you didn't want to see me after we'd made love."

"I—I was working," she hurriedly said.

He shot her a disbelieving look.

"I don't have answers to those questions, Tuck. Until I get my memory back, I can't tell you."

He said nothing.

"Is…is there anything else?"

"I don't know. Something was bothering you besides our relationship. You wouldn't talk about it."

She swallowed, her throat suddenly tight. This time she was the one who didn't speak.

Fortunately they'd reach Jessica and Cal's place. Tuck turned into the long driveway, pulling to a halt by Cal's truck. He got out of the car, but before he could reach the porch, the couple came out.

Cal was carrying a suitcase, a large thermos of coffee and a small ice chest. "She's packed enough to be gone a week," he grumbled as Tuck reached out to take the thermos and ice chest.

"I promise to bring her back in two days," Tuck said with a grin. After putting those items in the back seat, he stowed the suitcase in the trunk.

When Cal wrapped his arms around his wife, Tuck slid behind the wheel.

"This may take a minute," he whispered to Alex.

After a long goodbye kiss, Jessica started to get in the car, then noticed Alex's pillow and blanket. "What a good idea, Alex. Cal, I need a pillow and blanket, like Alex."

With a long-suffering sigh, Cal went back in the house and Jessica got in the back seat. "Mmm, your mother's sausage rolls. Terrific, Tuck."

"Don't credit me. Mom had them ready when I picked up the car this morning."

"I'm going to gain a lot of weight on this trip," Jessica said with a wicked grin that Alex enjoyed.

"All three of you ladies could probably handle a few more pounds. I know Doc wants Melanie to gain more weight. And Alex, here, certainly needs some extra pounds."

His caressing smile should have eased his criticism, but after their brief discussion, she knew not to take his attitude at face value. She'd heard the anger in his words.

Cal returned, handing the pillow and blanket to Jessica before offering her another prolonged goodbye kiss.

"Okay, Cal, that's enough," Tuck warned, "or we won't get to Dallas until dark."

Reluctantly, Cal closed the door. He looked at Tuck, whose window was down. "You be careful. And remind her to call me once you get there."

"Will do." Tuck backed out of the driveway before Cal decided to kiss his wife goodbye again.

They went through the same lengthy parting scene at Spence's, except Tuck recommended the pillow and blanket at once. That shortcut limited Spence to two goodbye kisses. But Maria, their housekeeper, had to say goodbye, also, and warn Tuck to be careful. Then Spence threatened Tuck with bodily harm if he drove too fast, reminded his wife to call him as soon as she arrived, and gave her instructions on getting rest and eating properly.

"Whew," Tuck said as they finally got on the road, "did you take notes, Melanie? He's a terrible mother hen."

"I know," Melanie agreed with a sigh, but she didn't sound unhappy to Alex. "But he loves me."

Those simple words, said with wonder and love, left them all silent. Alex recognized her emotion as envy. The confidence in Melanie's words and voice was worth more than anything on earth.

"I don't know about the rest of you, but I'm ready to eat," Jessica said, breaking the silence.

Since the car was full of the aroma of cinnamon and sausage rolls, everyone agreed.

FOUR HOURS LATER, Tuck checked the passengers in the back seat in his rearview mirror. They were as fast asleep as Alex next to him. After a hearty breakfast, and several bathroom stops, necessary with pregnant women, the three women had chatted among themselves. Then a few minutes ago, they'd all settled down for a little nap.

Finally, Tuck could think about the conversation he and Alex had had before picking up the other two. Should he have been so honest? After all, he was supposed to help keep Alex relaxed.

But it was hard to pretend everything was all right when he had so many questions. Right now, he wasn't even sure the baby was his. He thought it was. The Alex he'd known wouldn't have been sleeping with the other guy while the two of them were in a relationship.

But had it really been a relationship? He'd only seen her a few times. They'd gotten to the intimacy stage fairly quickly, but only because of the power of their touching. This morning, he could've carried her up the stairs, and he didn't think she would've protested.

In fact, it had been hard for him to back off. But he had, because that was what would be best for Alex. And because of those questions he had.

He thought of another question or two to ask Bill Parker. He might make a special phone call while the ladies were out shopping tomorrow. It might be better to ask those questions when Alex wasn't around.

Her two days in Cactus had brought some changes in her. She was no longer so pale, nor so tense. He'd heard her laugh several times. Only this morning, when faced with a return to Dallas, had her paleness and tension returned.

And that was why he'd had to come with her. To protect her while she was in Dallas. And to ensure her return to Cactus.

And as soon as she got back, he was going to get her an appointment with Doc Greenfield. All that tension couldn't be good for their baby.

His gaze returned to her smooth cheeks, now flushed with sleep. At least she was getting some rest now. Another hour or two and they'd be in Dallas.

"WE'RE HERE ALREADY?" Alex asked in surprise as she opened her eyes to find them parked outside her condo.

The two in the back seat stirred, stretching, too.

"Wow, that seemed a short ride," Jessica said. "What a charming town house, Alex."

"You never visited me?" she asked.

"No, we talked about me coming to Dallas, but I was so busy that I put it off. Then, none of us could find you after the wedding."

Melanie spoke up. "My mother-in-law, Edith, tried to invite you to our wedding, but you'd disappeared."

"That's probably about the time I went to D.C. I was there about a month before the accident."

"Did you usually work out of town that much?" Melanie asked. "I don't think I'd like that."

As a shiver coursed through her, Alex said, "I don't know. I don't think so, but I can't remember."

"You have your house keys?" Tuck asked. He'd popped the lid on the trunk and was about to get out to retrieve their bags.

"Oh, yes! I'll go unlock the door." Alex slid from the car, glad to stretch her legs. She was still a little groggy from her nap. She crossed to her front door, sliding the key into the door lock.

Funny, she wasn't panicky, as she'd been this morning, but she wasn't happy, either. Hadn't she liked living here? She stared at the town home complex for a moment, wondering about her previous life. When Bill had started his investigation, he'd talked to several neighbors, but he'd discovered she'd scarcely known any of them.

Except for Chad. He was the one who'd told her about the new town homes a year ago. He'd encouraged her to buy one—and then dropped by frequently, because he lived there, too. They'd become friends and then lovers, according to him.

But she didn't trust him.

"You got it open?" Tuck asked, startling her.

"Yes, of course," she said, turning the key and swinging open her front door. The decor wasn't a surprise. She'd lived here for the past month. But it wasn't welcoming, like Jessica's town house in Cactus.

"I—I'm not a very good housekeeper," she murmured apologetically as the two other women followed her in. Tuck, bringing up the rear with the luggage, laughed. "You've seen my house. I'm not, either."

"If you'd hire a housekeeper, like your mother has suggested, you wouldn't have to worry about it," Jessica pointed out. "You're both holding down full-time jobs. You're probably too tired at the end of the day to deal with dirty dishes and vacuuming."

"Yeah," Tuck agreed with a grin. Then he changed the subject immediately. "You two ladies find a phone and let your husbands know I got you here safely. I don't want them mad at me."

"There's a phone here in the kitchen," Alex said.

When Jessica and Melanie went to the phone, Tuck asked Alex where to put their bags. She led him up the stairs. "I have two bedrooms. I thought Jessica and Melanie could share my guest room."

As she walked by her own room, the answering

machine on her bedside table was flashing red. She tensed but passed it by.

Tuck set the bags inside the second bedroom and turned to face her. "What's wrong?" he asked at once.

"Wrong?"

"You seem upset."

"I have messages."

He studied her. "Afraid to listen to them?"

It seemed childish, but she nodded.

Taking her hand, he led her back to her bedroom. "Come on. I'll hold your hand while you listen. Bill might've called."

She was sure there was a call from Bill, but she figured Chad had left several messages, also. She hadn't told him when she was returning from Cactus, which hadn't pleased him.

Sucking in her breath, she pushed the play button on the machine.

"Alex, where are you? I thought you were going to stay home and rest. Call me." Chad's voice.

"Alex, it's almost midnight. Where are you?"

"Damn it, when are you coming home from that ridiculous little town. I told you what happened. Why didn't you believe me? I need to talk to you. Call me." Chad for the third time.

Tuck's hand squeezed hers, offering reassurance.

"Alex, I'm home safely and have talked to a couple more people. Give me a call when you come into town. Nothing urgent." Bill's voice was a comfort.

"Alex, I won't tolerate your behavior! I expect you to let me know where you are. After all, you're

carrying my baby. I shouldn't have to call some hayseed sheriff halfway across the state to find out
what's going on!'' Chad's frustrated voice.

"Cal's going to love that description," Tuck said
with a grin, "considering his years with the FBI here
in Dallas."

Since all the messages had been played, Alex
turned toward the door, glad to have that task completed. "I didn't know Cal had worked for the FBI.
Did I?"

"Don't know. We never discussed it. Cal wasn't
my favorite topic whenever I got close to you." His
smile reminded her of the kisses he'd given her. She
hurried for the door, anxious to join her friends.

"Alex?" Jessica called from downstairs. "Where
are you?"

"Up here. Come on up and I'll show you your
bedroom."

TUCK HEARD the relief in Alex's voice as she moved
to meet the ladies at the head of the stairs. Okay, so
maybe he'd pushed it a little last night and this
morning. But it was hard to be around her without
touching. And touching led to kissing. And kissing
would lead to a bed if they indulged in much more.

"Ladies, while you're settling in, I'll go find a
hotel room. Do you want to shop this afternoon, or
have an early dinner, take in a movie and go to bed
at a reasonable time?"

"O-oh! A first-run movie. That sounds fun," Jessica said. "And even though we napped, I don't
want a late night. How does that sound to you?"
she asked the other two.

The vote was unanimous. He promised to buy a paper and scope out what was playing. After promising to be back by five-thirty, he left.

He found a chain hotel nearby and got a room for two nights. After buying a newspaper in the lobby, he carried his bag to the room.

Throwing it on the bed, he went immediately to the phone, pulling out the business card Bill had given him.

"Bill, Tuck here. How's it going?"

"Fine. You in Dallas?"

"Yeah." He gave him his hotel number.

"So, Alex is at her condo alone?"

"Nope. That didn't seem like a good idea to me. So Jessica and Melanie came, and we're turning it into a two-day shopping trip."

"Ah, good."

"You think Lowery is going to cause trouble?"

"Possibly. He lives in the same complex with Alex. I'm sure he'll call her once he realizes she's back. He called me this morning, demanding information. When I refused to tell him anything, he thought he could threaten me with a lawsuit, typical lawyer stuff."

"There were several messages on her answering machine."

"I figured."

"Have you found out anything else?"

"Not really. One woman lawyer at the office volunteered that Lowery was after her hot and heavy. But this lady said she didn't think he and Alex had ever gotten together."

That thought cheered Tuck. "Good. Listen, I wanted to ask you something."

"I don't know if I can answer."

"I know. But...but something was bothering Alex. I don't know if it was Lowery, her job, or what. You got any ideas?"

"Maybe."

Chapter Seven

When the investigator said nothing else, Tuck demanded, "Well? Are you going to tell me?"

"Look, Langford, all I have are impressions, speculation. No facts."

"I understand, but something was bothering Alex before she lost her memory. Only we didn't do a lot of talking when we were alone."

"Understood. She's a beautiful woman."

Tuck tamped down the immediate flare of jealousy. He'd seen Bill Parker with Alex. The man treated her like a daughter. "Tell me what your impression of the situation was."

"What do you know about Alex's father?"

"Her father? He's dead." Tuck was confused by the change of subject. "I want to know about Alex, not—"

"Let me make my point. Alex was the only child of one of the most famous and prestigious attorneys in the history of Dallas. Big shoes to fill."

"You think her father put pressure on her?"

"No. I suspect he pretty much ignored her except for encouraging her law career. Her mother died when Alex was seventeen. I think both she and her mother had to compete with her father's career for any attention.''

"Okay." What could he say?

"When I escorted Alex to the office to do interviews, I noticed she tensed up immediately. At first I thought it was Lowery. And he does make her tense, by the way, though not the way you do.''

"Good."

"Yeah, I thought you'd like to hear that," the older man said with a chuckle. Then his voice grew serious again. "But then we went to the office when she knew Lowery was out of town. Same problem.''

"So you think something at work isn't right?"

"I think Alex is disillusioned with the cynical behavior of lawyers. I think, for her father, she pursued a law career, made it the center of her life, as her father did, and now isn't happy with it.''

"That's a lot of supposition," Tuck said slowly, thinking about what the man had said.

"I warned you.''

"Yeah."

"Anyway, keep an eye out for Lowery. He'll upset Alex. The man has no class.''

"I'm glad Jessica and Melanie are with her. I'll get back over there at once.''

"The man's not dangerous. But he'll raise her stress level.''

"Yeah. Thanks, Bill.''

"As far as I'm concerned, we never talked.''

"Right."

Tuck hung up the phone, found the entertainment section of the paper, tucked it under his arm, and headed for the door. He wasn't going to leave the ladies there alone if he could help it.

ALEX REVELED in Jessica's and Melanie's company. Sometimes it seemed to her she was always alone. But these two women were becoming good friends, apparently for the second time. And they laughed so much.

Tuck had said he'd be back about five-thirty or six, and the three of them each took a shower, gave each other manicures and talked about mundane things, pleasant things. They each told her about their lives in Cactus, and she longed to return to the small town.

"We were surprised that a sophisticated Dallas lawyer took to our town so much, but we were pleased," Jessica said.

"Don't make it sound like you're all hicks," Alex said. "You're both running your own businesses."

"Yeah," Melanie said with a smile. "But unlike Jess, I'm not making a profit."

They all laughed, the other two assuring Melanie that it took a while to get established.

When the doorbell sounded, Alex checked her watch. Five o'clock was too soon for Tuck. She tensed, fearing Chad had left the office early, for once in his life, and discovered her arrival.

"What's wrong? It's probably Tuck," Jessica said, staring at her.

"If it is, he's half an hour early."

"He probably couldn't stay away from you any longer," Melanie suggested, grinning. "Every time he looks at you, I think he's going to take a bite out of you."

Alex blushed and reluctantly went to answer the door.

When she discovered an impatient Tuck there, she smiled in relief. "Oh, I'm glad it's you."

"Me, too. Why didn't you tell me Lowery lived here?"

Jessica and Melanie had followed Alex.

"That man lives with you?" Jessica asked with a gasp. Both ladies looked shocked.

"No!" Alex returned. "Tuck means he lives in this complex."

"Wow. That threw me for a loop, Tuck," Jessica said with a chuckle.

"She should've told me."

Melanie stepped forward, studying Tuck. "You're acting like this guy is dangerous. Would he hurt Alex?"

"No, of course not!" Alex answered instead of Tuck. "He might bore me to death, but he wouldn't hurt me." Suddenly it occurred to Alex to wonder how Tuck had discovered where Chad lived. When she asked him, he didn't answer immediately.

"Well? You're complaining that I didn't tell you, so it wasn't me. Who did tell you?"

"Uh, Bill," he said hurriedly before pulling the paper from under his arm. "We need to decide what movie we're going to see. Do you like action, comedy, what?"

"Did you call Bill?" Alex asked, not at all distracted.

Tuck tried again. "Yeah. What do you think,

ladies?'' He opened the paper and began reading the names of movies.

Alex crossed her arms over her chest and stared at him. ''Don't you think *I* should've been the one to talk to Bill, since he's in my employ?''

Tuck gave up the fight. Putting the paper down on the coffee table, he put his hands on his hips and glared at her. ''Yeah, you should've been. But you didn't call him. What were you doing?''

''We were doing our nails,'' Jessica informed him, grinning. ''Don't you love the color Alex chose?''

''Doing your nails? We came to Dallas to—''

''To pack up some clothes,'' Alex reminded him. ''I said I'd call Bill, but I do have two days.''

''We also came to relax, Tuck,'' Melanie reminded him with a gentle smile. ''Alex is supposed to stay relaxed.''

Alex liked having her friends there to support her. If she and Tuck had been alone, she suspected he would've continued to argue. But Melanie's words shut him up at once.

He smiled with all his considerable charm. ''Sorry, I forgot. Well, then, I suggest a comedy. How about this one?'' he asked, pointing to an ad.

''That's a man's movie,'' Jessica said in dismissal. ''Here's a romantic comedy. How about that?''

Tuck seemed to be getting into the spirit of things as he moaned in protest, grinning all the while. ''That's a date movie.''

Alex actually found herself laughing as she leaned forward and kissed his cheek. ''And you've got three dates, so it's perfect. What time does it start, Jess?''

''Seven-fifteen. We can have an early dinner, see the movie and be home by ten. Perfect.''

Alex agreed. She couldn't remember the last time she'd blown an evening at dinner and the movies. Then she grinned even wider. Of course she couldn't. She couldn't remember what she used to do with her evenings.

THE EVENING WAS A SUCCESS as far as Tuck was concerned. The food had been good, the movie funny, and he'd held Alex's hand in the dark.

Now, driving back to Alex's town house, all three ladies were beginning to sound drowsy.

''Is it normal for pregnant ladies to sleep as much as this?'' Tuck asked.

''Yes!'' came the resounding answer from all three.

''Hey, don't shoot me for asking. I've never been around pregnant women before. At least, I didn't know I was.'' He gestured to Jessica and Melanie in the back seat. ''These two didn't tell anyone they were pregnant until the night you arrived.''

''We thought it better to keep it a secret because of your mothers,'' Melanie reminded him.

''That silly bet,'' Tuck said. ''Cal and Spence's mothers really worked at getting those two married, but my mom hasn't bothered me too much. She introduced a few ladies to me, but that didn't bother me.''

''No. Too many women has never been a problem

for you,'' Jessica said. She'd known him almost as long as she'd known Cal.

''Oh?'' Alex said, sitting up straighter and staring at Tuck. ''Were you socially active while I was losing my memory?''

''You mean, did I sleep with anyone? That's what you want to know, isn't it?'' His good humor seemed to have disappeared.

But Alex didn't back down. ''Yes, that's what I want to know. I should've asked right away if you'd found someone else. But since I'm so confused about what happened, I didn't. Have you?''

''Have I found someone else that I'm interested in? No.''

The two in the back seat said nothing, and Tuck thought maybe they could save this conversation until they were alone. But apparently Alex didn't agree.

In a soft voice she said, ''And the other question? Have you slept with anyone?''

''Have you?'' After all, it had been a month since she had lost her memory.

''No. I haven't. And you?''

''No!'' he snapped. It wasn't that he hadn't tried. There had been a period of time when he'd thought quantity might help him forget the quality he'd lost. But he hadn't been able to generate enough interest in any other woman.

He didn't know what he expected from her in the way of reaction, but she smiled at him and reached over to squeeze his hand as it rested on his thigh.

He thought he was going to run the car right off the road.

"Careful," she murmured, still smiling.

"Uh, yeah," he agreed, all the while wondering if he could get her alone for a good-night kiss.

He parked the Cadillac in front of her condo, and everyone got out. Alex preceded the others to unlock the door. Just as she shoved it open, a man called her name.

Tuck turned around and watched him as he jogged across the parking lot. It had to be Chad Lowery. Not bad-looking, if you liked the preppy type with narrow eyes.

"It's about time you got home. Why did you stay so long? You belong here," the man insisted as he approached Alex.

Tuck stepped in front of him.

"Get out of my way."

Tuck crossed his arms over his chest. "Nope. Alex is tired. She doesn't have time for visitors tonight."

"It looks like she has too many visitors, especially you. Alex, tell this hayseed to let me by."

"No, I don't think so. Tuck is right. I'm too tired to talk to you tonight." She spoke calmly.

"Are you coming to the office tomorrow?"

"No, I haven't recovered my memory. We're going shopping. Good night, Chad."

"Alex!" he protested as she walked up the stairs inside her condo. She didn't hesitate, and he tried to push past Tuck.

"You heard her," Tuck said, shoving the man's shoulders.

"Touch me again, and I'll have you arrested for assault and battery."

"Typical lawyer, threatening to sue everyone. I'm on private property, and you're trespassing."

"I'm trying to speak to my future wife."

Tuck felt the anger rise in him. "She's *my* future wife, not yours, and that baby is mine, too. So leave her alone."

Lowery paled. "You're claiming to be the father of her baby? Don't be ridiculous. She's only known you— I mean, you live in Cactus, don't you? She only made a couple of quick trips out there. She wouldn't have— You're taking advantage of her, hoping to cash in, aren't you?"

"Cash in?" Tuck asked, staring at the other man.

"Don't pretend like you don't know! Alex is worth a lot of money." He looked at Tuck's clothing and laughed scornfully. "Everyone will call you a fortune hunter. It's obvious you don't have much money."

Tuck looked down at his jeans, shirt and three-hundred-dollar boots. Then he thoroughly inspected the other man's tailored suit, silk tie, Rolex watch. There was definitely a difference in their dress.

"Is that what you're doing? Trying to cash in?" he asked softly, watching the other man's face.

It turned bright red. "How dare you!" he screeched.

Just then the door opened again. "Tuck, are you coming in?" Alex asked calmly.

"Alex," Chad began at once.

"Yep, I am," Tuck said, and sauntered inside, enjoying Lowery's anger and frustration.

"Alexandra, I must talk to you!"

She smiled. "Not tonight. Goodbye, Chad." And she shut the door.

"Good job, lady," Tuck said as he wrapped his arms around her. He recognized at once that her calm was only skin deep. She was tense, unable to relax against him. Time for a cure.

He lowered his lips to hers, feeding the hunger that had grown all evening. As a distraction, kissing worked just fine, except that he wanted more.

"Lordy, lordy, you do pack a punch, Miss Alex," he whispered in her ear when he finally lifted his lips from hers.

"You've said that before, cowboy," she returned, tightening her hold around his neck. "But I told you it's not me. It's you."

"Yes, you did," he agreed, "but I didn't know you could remember it."

Her smile disappeared and she stared at him. "I— I did remember, didn't I? I remembered!"

"Well, don't get in a state. It wasn't that big a memory," he told her with a grin.

"But I remembered!"

"Hey, I've got an idea."

"What?" she asked, but he could tell she was distracted, her mind racing as she tried to dredge up more memories.

"I think we should sleep together to see if you can remember anything else. Just for the sake of science, you understand."

She laughed, still pleased at her memory, but she shook her head no, much to his chagrin. "I don't think so, cowboy, but it *is* an original line."

"Everything all right?" Jessica called down the stairs.

Alex pulled away from Tuck and crossed the hall. "Everything's fine. And I even remembered something."

Both ladies came down the stairs in a rush. "What?" Jessica demanded. "What did you remember?"

"Did you remember who—" Melanie began, but Alex shook her head.

"Nothing so dramatic. But I told Tuck that he'd said—something before, and he had. And I remembered it."

You would've thought she'd remembered the formula for a great medical cure, Tuck thought with a grin. She was beaming. But even if it was a minor thing, it made her believe things would come right.

With time.

And a lot of kisses. And he was willing to sacrifice himself for Alex's memory. Oh, yeah, he'd be first in line.

After all the congratulations, Jessica looked at Tuck. "What are you still doing here? We're ready to go to bed."

"Me, too," Tuck said, and waggled his eyebrows at Alex.

Melanie giggled. "I bet you've heard that before, too, Alex."

All three ladies laughed, and Tuck shook his head in disgust. "Okay, okay, I'm going. But don't open the door to that sleaze lawyer, you hear me, Alex?"

"I told you he isn't dangerous."

"Maybe not, but I don't want him upsetting you."

"We'll protect her," Melanie assured him.

Jessica nodded.

"Then I guess I'll go." He looked at his friends' wives, but they didn't take the hint. Finally he leaned forward and briefly kissed Alex, wanting more. "Sure you don't want to come see my hotel room? It's real nice."

Jessica grinned and answered his question, as if it were directed at her. "Gee, thanks, Tuck, but Cal doesn't like me to go to hotel rooms with other men."

"Good, 'cause I wasn't inviting you."

Alex laughed. "Go away, Tuck. We'll see you in the morning."

"What are our plans?" he asked, hoping to prolong the parting.

"We're going shopping, remember?" Melanie said.

"For baby things? I don't know much—"

"No," Jessica assured him. "We can buy things for the babies later, in Lubbock. We can even find some things in Cactus. We're going shopping for maternity clothes tomorrow. They have some great shops here in Dallas."

"You won't mind taking us, will you?" Alex asked, suddenly realizing a day spent shopping for maternity clothes might not be his favorite thing.

"Nah, I don't mind," he assured her. He would've have promised to walk on hot coals, if Alex had asked him. But it did occur to him he might receive a few strange looks toting three pregnant ladies around town tomorrow.

With the way things were going, he'd probably be arrested for polygamy.

Chapter Eight

Alex slept like a baby.

Until a loud pounding on her front door awakened her at seven-thirty the next morning.

She threw on her robe and started downstairs. Before she got far, Jessica called to her. "Alex? Who is it?"

"I don't know," she called over her shoulder. "Probably Chad." She ignored the whispering between Jessica and Melanie and hurried down the stairs before the pounding gave her a headache.

Swinging open the door, she glared at the elegantly dressed man. "Do you have any idea what time it is?"

"Of course I do," Chad Lowery assured her. "Why did you take so long to answer?"

"I was asleep."

"You should be up by now. You're used to getting up early."

She wanted to slap him. "Chad, I'm pregnant, and I need more sleep. I'm not going to work this morning. And what I do is my business, not yours."

He stiffened. "I think it could be considered my business since we're going to be married soon."

"It doesn't matter how often you say those words, they're not going to happen," she said firmly. "I don't know what we shared in the past, but we share nothing now. Even if this is your baby, I'm not going to marry you."

"Then I'll sue for custody!" he snapped.

She studied him, considering his threat. Then she asked a simple question. "Why?"

He became flustered, his face turning red. "Because it's my child."

Suddenly something clicked into place for Alex. "And you'd sue for child support, right?"

He looked as if he was going to choke. "That would only be fair!"

"And if I keep custody, you'll pay child support?"

"I would offer any support you need, of course, but with your inheritance and interest in the firm, I don't think you'll need—"

"Go away, Chad. I'll let you know when I recover my memory." She shut the door in his face even as he protested.

She turned away, ignoring his continued appeal for her to open the door, only to discover Jessica and Melanie standing in the hall wrapped in their robes.

"Are you okay?" Jessica asked.

"Of course. But thanks for being here."

"Um, I have a confession to make," Jessica said. "I called Tuck when you said it was Chad pounding on the door. He sounded pretty violent."

"Oh, dear. Call and see if he's left yet," Alex pleaded. "I don't want—"

Angry male voices sounded outside the door.

Alex ran to pull the door open again, hoping she wouldn't be breaking up a fight.

"Get away from that door!" Tuck shouted at Lowery.

"Don't touch me!" Lowery yelled in return, backing away from Tuck.

"I won't if you stay away from Alex."

"I have as much right as you to talk to her."

"Not when I tell you to stay away."

"You can't—"

The door opened and Tuck saw Alex's beautiful face over Lowery's shoulder. "Morning, sweetheart. I found some garbage on your front porch."

"Tuck, don't pick a fight," she warned sternly. "Chad was just leaving."

Lowery immediately gave lie to her words. "Alex, you have to let me explain."

"Goodbye, Chad. I'll let you know."

Tuck stood there, his hands on his hips, staring at the man in the expensive silk suit and power tie. If he didn't leave, as Alex wanted him to do, Tuck would delight in showing the man some of his own power.

"I'm going to file suit for custody," Lowery informed Alex and then turned to step around Tuck on the way to his car.

"What's he talking about?" Tuck asked as he stepped to the porch and swept a disheveled Alex into a warm embrace. Man, she felt good in his arms.

As natural as rain on a spring day, she raised her lips for a kiss. Tuck was happy to oblige.

"All right, you two, you're making us miss our husbands," Melanie complained.

Tuck raised his head to stare at the impromptu audience. "Hey, I didn't ask you to join us."

Jessica grinned. "We called you, Tuck. You owe us for that."

"Yeah," he agreed, grinning in return. "Now, explain what he meant," he demanded, looking down at Alex.

She shrugged out of his arms and headed for the kitchen. "I need my cup of tea. Jessica? Melanie?"

"Tea? What about coffee? And what about the answer to my question?" Tuck called, following her.

"I'll explain, but I can do that and fix tea and coffee at the same time."

Everyone piled into the kitchen and soon they all had cups in front of them. Tuck didn't push her until Alex joined him at the table. "Well?"

"He's threatening to sue for custody of the baby."

Tuck had been about to sip his coffee, but he slammed the cup into the saucer, his coffee sloshing over the edges. "He's about to do what?"

"Sue for custody—"

"It's not his baby!" Tuck shouted.

Jessica laid a hand on Tuck's forearm. "Calm down."

Melanie cocked her head to one side and looked at Alex. "Why has he decided to do that?"

"It suddenly struck me, when he first threatened the suit, that it wasn't the baby he wanted. It was money," Alex explained. "You see, I—I have a lot of money."

"I guess you do get a good salary," Jessica said. "I've heard big-time lawyers make a lot."

Tuck watched her try to hide her embarrassment, and he fought the urge to pull her into his lap for a cuddle. A sudden picture of a little blond girl, looking exactly like Alex, his little girl, distracted him from his anger.

"It's more than that. My father was very wealthy. As an only child, I inherited his money plus half interest in the law firm where I work."

"And you think he's after your money?" Jessica asked. "What a charmer."

"Well, he admitted he'd expect child support, but he didn't think he'd need to pay any if I had custody."

"You'll have custody, all right," Tuck assured her, cupping her cheek with his hand. "With me. Because that baby is mine."

"I hope you're right," Alex admitted.

Tuck leaned forward and kissed her warm lips. He was beyond words. When one of the other ladies cleared her throat, he didn't know which one, he reluctantly withdrew his mouth from Alex's. But he whispered, "Let's get married while we're in Dallas."

"No."

Alex's response was like a dash of cold water in his face. "But you said—"

"I said I hope my child is yours, but I'm not going to marry anyone until I know for sure."

Her gaze pleaded with Tuck to understand, and he fought back his indignation. He believed this was his baby, but he admitted he wanted to know for sure. But in the end, he was going to marry Alex anyway. So he'd wait.

"Why don't you ladies go get dressed while I fix breakfast?" he asked, his voice even.

"You're not angry?"

"Nope. When you recover your memory, we'll get married."

"I didn't say I'd marry you," Alex said, suddenly backtracking.

"Get dressed," he ordered.

"Tuck, we didn't do any grocery shopping," Melanie reminded him.

"Okay, I'll wait down here until you're dressed and we'll go to IHOP."

"Mmm, pancakes!" Jessica said with enthusiasm. She started immediately for the stairs. Melanie grinned in anticipation and followed Jessica.

Alex didn't budge.

"You're mad at me."

Tuck pulled her against him, his lips tracing her neck. "No, sweetheart, I'm not mad. Maybe irritated a little. But you've always been hardheaded. No reason I should think you would change, just because you lost your memory."

"So I haven't changed?" she asked, a hopeful expression on her beautiful face.

He could give her nothing but the truth. "You've changed, a little," he added, as disappointment filled her expression. "You used to be more...confident. That's all. And you've shown flashes of your old self. But you're no less beautiful...or desirable."

Her gaze shone with the moisture of sudden tears, and a tremulous smile made him yearn to kiss her, but before he could close the distance between them, she whispered a thank-you and raced up the stairs.

Shoving his hand into his jeans pockets, Tuck turned back to the kitchen to finish his cup of coffee. He'd already had his shower and shaved, since he had risen early, as all ranchers did.

Now all he had to do was wait for the three pregnant ladies abovestairs to reappear so he could escort them to breakfast and satisfy at least *one* of his hungers.

RUTH LANGFORD couldn't resist calling her friends.

"Tuck has gone to Dallas with Alex," she told Mabel Baxter.

"I know. Jessica and Melanie went with them. Cal's beside himself worrying about her."

"Tuck will keep them all safe. But I agree, they shouldn't have gone with Tuck and Alex. They don't need chaperones."

"Jessica said they went because with Alex's memory loss, she didn't need any pressure from Tuck."

Ruth squared her jaw. "Tuck would never do anything to hurt Alex. I—I think he's in love with her." She couldn't keep the hopefulness that filled her out of her voice.

"That's wonderful," Mabel said.

After basically the same conversation with Edith, Ruth added, "I know I probably won't win the contest, but until Jessica and Melanie turn up pregnant, I can still hope."

"Of course you can," Edith agreed. "With those two working on their careers, who knows when the first baby will arrive."

"And, mostly, I want Tuck to be happy. He's changed a lot since Alex came back to town."

Florence was just as supportive as Ruth's other two friends, though an underlying sadness was apparent.

"Maybe Mac will find someone suddenly," Ruth consoled.

"She could drive into town with neon lights flashing 'I love you, Mac,' and he'd look the other way. I don't know what I'm going to do, Ruth," Florence said in despair.

"I know. I felt the same way until Alex came back. If she leaves again—well, I hope she and Tuck stay together, even if my son leaves Cactus, which would break my heart. But not as much as it would if he stayed alone, unhappy, the way he's been the last couple of months."

"I don't know that you could say he was alone," Florence reminded her.

"Oh, I know there were women, but—"

"Yeah. At least there were women. Mac is just alone. And now, with all three of his friends' lives centered around their women, he's really alone."

Ruth, after hanging up the phone, gave thanks that

Tuck had rediscovered Alex, no matter what happened.

Poor Florence.

AGAIN, on the drive back, the three ladies took a long nap. Tuck could understand their sleeping a little better this time. He'd found the all-day shopping spree exhausting himself.

Of course, he hadn't actually done any shopping. He'd followed the three women, carried tons of bags, and made periodic trips out to the car to stash the latest purchases in the trunk.

There had been a few strange looks from the sales ladies as they realized all three women were at about the same stage in their pregnancies and all three had trooped out of the dressing rooms to ask his opinion.

As if he knew anything about maternity clothes.

Everything Alex put on looked wonderful to him. When she'd ask if the clothes made her look fat, he'd known the right answer. After all, he wasn't stupid.

And he'd performed the same service for his friends' wives. All three ladies had bought a lot of clothes and been happy. Alex seemed even more relaxed, once Chad Lowery had been vanquished. She'd had a conversation with Bill that encouraged her to believe she'd recover her memory soon.

Tuck hoped so. He wanted to claim Alex as his own. And that wouldn't happen until she did remember.

Still, he wasn't going to stop trying to persuade her to marry him. He intended to ask her to move out to his ranch instead of going to the condo. She'd accepted his kisses, even encouraged them. He thought it was time to move to the next level.

Jessica and Melanie had called ahead to tell their husbands when they'd reach town. The men had told them to come to Cal's office. Tuck awakened his sleeping beauties as they approached Cactus, and Jessica and Melanie quickly combed their hair and powdered their noses to look good for their husbands.

Tuck could've told them such care wasn't necessary. He found Alex's sleep-tousled beauty to be irresistible. When he pulled up in front of the sheriff's office, he put the car in park and pulled Alex close for a kiss.

"What was that for?" she asked, her voice breathless.

"I was hungry," he muttered, staring at her.

Cal and Spence immediately appeared and helped their wives out of the car, each engaging in a similar activity. Cal wrapped his arm around Jessica's shoulders and started for his office.

Tuck opened the door. "Wait a minute, pal. You're not going anywhere without your wife's packages. You, too, Spence." He moved to the back of the car and opened the trunk, now jammed with shopping bags as well as their luggage.

Both men turned to stare.

"What did you do, buy out all the stores in Dallas?" Cal asked.

"Only half of them," Jessica assured him with another kiss. Which clearly erased any complaints he might've been about to make.

Alex got out of the car and the three ladies began sorting out their purchases.

"You're back!" Mabel called.

Everyone turned to see her and Ruth crossing the square. There were hugs all around before Ruth reminded them of their secret.

"You bought a lot. I can't wait to see what's fashionable now. I haven't been to Dallas in a couple of years. Let's see what you bought."

Jessica, Melanie and Alex all looked at each other helplessly. Cal and Spence realized something was wrong, but they weren't aware that all their wives' purchases would reveal the secret of their pregnancies.

Tuck recognized the difficulty at once. "Not here on the street, Mom. Maybe later. These three are kind of tired."

"Oh, of course. How silly of me. Why don't we barbecue tonight and everyone come for dinner? Then we can hear all about your trip," Ruth said, an excited smile on her face.

"Great idea," Mabel agreed. "I'll fix—"

"Um, Mom," Cal interrupted, his face red. "I was kind of looking forward to having Jessica to myself tonight."

"Oh," Mabel said, her eyes rounding.

Ruth said, "I guess the rest of you feel the same way. Sorry, I didn't think."

"Tuck and I would love to come." Alex spoke up, smiling at Ruth. "I'd have to grocery shop before I could cook, and I'm a little tired."

Ruth beamed at her. "Wonderful. We'll make it

just family tonight and have a celebration another time.''

Tuck was about to protest the decision being made for him when Alex said, ''I—I'm not family, Ruth.''

Immediately his objections disappeared. Sliding his arm around her shoulders, he pulled her close. ''Close as family. Mom's never had a daughter. You can let her adopt you.''

Nodding, Ruth continued to smile at Alex. ''Is there anything you don't like to eat?''

''No, nothing. And I'm starving. You're sure you don't mind cooking for us?''

Everyone around them laughed. Tuck squeezed Alex's shoulders at her startled look at the others.

''Sweetheart, Mom loves to cook for people. She used to encourage me to bring home all my friends so she could feed them. Cal, Spence and Mac ate half their meals at my house.''

Spence added, ''Our moms kind of shared the four of us since they all wanted more kids. Sometimes we had several dinners in one day.''

Amid the laughter, Ruth kissed her son and then Alex goodbye, telling them to come over whenever they were ready. Dinner would be served about seven.

''Whew, that was close,'' Jessica said when Ruth and Mabel returned to their cars.

''What, having dinner out?'' Cal asked.

''No, showing them our purchases. All we bought were maternity clothes.''

''Ssh!'' Melanie warned as several ladies walked by, greeting them.

"So when are we going to tell them?" Spence asked. "I feel guilty for keeping quiet. They'll be so excited."

"I know," Jessica agreed, "but let's try to keep it a secret another week or two."

Tuck caught Jessica's sideways look at him and Alex. Well, he was going to do his part to speed things up. "Let's take everything over to the condo," he suggested to Alex. "Then we ought to do a little grocery shopping while I'm here to help you." Unless, of course, he convinced her to move in with him.

"Okay. Thanks for going with us," she told Jessica and Melanie, kissing each one on the cheek.

"We had fun," Melanie assured her. "Let us know if you need anything for the condo."

"Yeah, we'll be checking on you," Jessica added. "We've got your cell phone number."

Tuck waited until all the goodbyes were spoken and then helped Alex back into the front seat. When they drove off, it was their first time to be alone in several days.

"I'm glad Jess and Mel went with us, but I'm glad we're finally alone again," he said, smiling.

Alex offered no comment.

He turned to frown at her. "Alex?"

"Yes?"

"Are you unhappy that we're alone?"

"No, of course not." She ran a finger over the upholstery as if she'd never been in the car before, instead of having spent two days traveling in it.

He pulled into the driveway of the condo. "Is something bothering you?"

"No."

"Okay. Then how about we skip the condo and move you into my house? Once we're married you'll be living there anyway, so it will be simpler—"

"You sound just like Chad."

Her statement hit him like a slap in the face. "What did you say?"

"I said you sound—"

"Never mind. I heard it the first time. Why would you insult me like that?"

"I didn't mean it as an insult. But it's the truth."

"Why?"

She turned and stared at him. "You're assuming I'm going to marry you."

"It's my baby," he said insistently, thinking he'd already fought this battle.

"Maybe. But that still doesn't mean I'm going to marry you."

Chapter Nine

Tuck frowned, staring at her.

"Wait a minute. I'm confused. I know you said you weren't going to make a decision until you got your memory back. But once we know the baby is mine, we'll be married. And I know the baby is mine."

"No, you don't. And what I do after I know who the daddy is hasn't been decided. So I'll stay right here in the condo."

"Why won't you agree to marry me if the baby is mine?"

She opened the car door and got out. She really didn't want to have this discussion now. But Tuck got out of the car, too, as she'd expected.

"We haven't known each other all that long. And I don't know how our life-styles will fit together. I live in Dallas."

"And I don't. But you're not happy in Dallas."

"I don't know what I am. I don't even know who I am. I'm a stranger everywhere." It was a frightening thought, one that she'd held at bay as long as

Jessica and Melanie were with her. Now she was on her own.

Without a car.

Suddenly she felt terminally stupid. "Why didn't I bring my car back?"

"Car? We're talking about—"

"I know," she agreed with a sigh, "but right now talking about what I'm going to do when I get my memory back won't solve anything. But the fact that I left my car in Dallas affects everything. I should've driven it back here."

"I'll take you wherever you want to go."

"I can't ask that of you. You have work to do."

She saw the tug-of-war in his eyes and smiled. "Don't worry. I'll figure out something."

He appeared frustrated with her independence. "Nope, you haven't changed at all." He turned to the back of the car and started unloading her bag and her purchases. "Go unlock the door," he ordered.

She thought about collecting some of her shopping bags, but the glare he sent her warned her of trouble. She'd give him control of the unloading. Maybe it would make him feel better. A smile danced across her lips as she remembered Tuck's determination every time they were together. He wanted her to depend on him.

"What are you smiling about?" he said with a growl.

"I was remembering your stubbornness," she said. "You always insisted on being the one in charge. Sometimes I thought you were herding me, like you do the cows."

He didn't smile. Instead his eyes narrowed, and he said softly, "You remembered?"

TUCK RETURNED his mother's car after he'd carried in all of Alex's belongings.

"Did you have a good time in Dallas?" she asked as soon as he entered the house.

"Sure. Fine." His mind was on Alex and her memory, coupled with her stubbornness.

"You don't sound happy," Ruth said, staring at him.

He shrugged his shoulders just as his father walked in. "Alex keeps refusing to marry me."

"So?" Frank asked, with no concern.

"I don't know if I can convince her," Tuck almost shouted, frustrated.

"No son of mine would give up just because he got a no the first time he asked," Frank said, a smile on his face. "Did you think your mother accepted my first proposal?"

Tuck turned startled eyes on his mother.

She lifted her nose in the air. "I needed time to think."

"Hell, woman, it took you an entire month to change your mind," Frank roared.

"I had to be sure you meant it. You were quite a womanizer in your younger days. I wasn't going to have a husband who played around."

Tuck stared at both his parents, stunned by their revelations. He'd always seen them as his parents, not as a couple trying to reconcile their differences.

"Dad? A womanizer?"

His mother turned her gaze to him, her eyebrows

raised. "Where do you think you got it from, Tucker Langford? Not *my* side of the family."

Tuck and his father shared a smile. "So how did you convince her, Dad?"

"I crawled along behind her, ready to propose at a moment's notice, for all thirty of those days. I didn't look at another woman."

"I've already done that," Tuck reminded him.

"Not for thirty days. But you keep at it, son. She'll come around. We Langfords are hard to resist."

Ruth leaned over and kissed her husband's cheek. "He's right about that."

ALEX WAS STRETCHED OUT on her bed, resting before she dressed for dinner, when her cell phone rang.

She answered it reluctantly, fearing it would be Chad pleading his case one more time.

Instead she heard Mac's voice. "Alex? Is Tuck there?"

"No, Mac, he's gone home."

"No, I tried his house."

"Oh, he probably went to his parents' house to return his mother's car."

"Thanks, I'll call him there. By the way, welcome back."

"Thanks," she said with a little sigh.

"When are you coming to the office? I could use some help."

"Well, I have to go into Lubbock in the morning, but—"

"So do I," Mac said in surprise.

"You do? I don't suppose I could bum a ride?" Alex asked, delighted to have maybe found a way to solve her problem.

"Sure you could, but I'll be there until after lunch. Will that be too long for you?"

"Probably not. I'm going to buy a car, so I may be able to get back on my own." She'd decided buying a car was the only choice she had.

"Buying a car? You didn't bring your car from Dallas?" Mac asked, surprise in his voice.

"I'm afraid I didn't think about it."

"Wouldn't it be cheaper to hire someone to drive your car out here?"

"Maybe, but I've been thinking of trading it in anyway. It will be faster to buy what I want now, and sell my car when I get back to Dallas."

"Then I'll pick you up in the morning, about eight-thirty, if that's okay," Mac agreed. "It'll be nice to have the company."

"That would be wonderful. Thanks, Mac."

Well, that problem was solved, she thought as she lay back down. She'd been wondering if Cactus had a taxi. She didn't want to ask Tuck to drive her. He'd already spent three days away from his ranch for her.

She didn't want to rely on Tuck too much. He seemed to assume her compliance about marriage if she let him take care of her.

Which reminded her, she hadn't made a trip to the grocery store. Maybe she could get Tuck to stop for some milk on the way home tonight.

The doorbell rang.

She checked her watch. It was only five-thirty and

Tuck had said he'd be back at six-thirty. Had someone else decided to drop by? At least she knew it wouldn't be Chad this time. He wouldn't make the long drive.

When she opened the door, Tuck was waiting for her, his long muscled body propped against the brick wall.

"I thought you said six-thirty?" she asked.

He grinned. "I did. But then we forgot to do any grocery shopping for you, so I came back earlier."

"I can—"

"No arguments," he said, moving forward until he was close enough to kiss her. Which he did.

"I'm not dressed," she added once he lifted his lips from hers. She tugged the edges of her robe closer together.

"I'll wait, unless you want to invite me up to watch," he suggested, waggling his eyebrows.

She gave him her sternest lawyer look, but her lips quivered with laughter at his teasing, so she didn't think she scared him. "No, I won't invite you to watch. But I'll hurry. Thank you for remembering."

"My pleasure."

She hurried up the stairs before she could give in to his charm.

When she came back down the stairs, she was wearing one of her new purchases. The long maroon sweater and leggings resembled outfits she'd seen in the stores for the non-pregnant customer.

"Wow. You look terrific," Tuck said when she came into sight.

"You don't think it looks like a maternity out-fit?"

"Nope."

"My stomach doesn't stick out too far?"

He reached out and rubbed his big hand over her stomach. "No. Even if the sweater were tight, I don't think anyone could tell, but the sweater is loose. Shouldn't you be getting bigger by now?"

"I don't know. I have good stomach muscles be-cause I always exercise. Wouldn't that make a dif-ference?"

"I don't know. We need to make you an appoint-ment with Doc. I'll call in the morning and—"

"I'll do the calling for my appointment," she as-sured him crisply.

"Okay, first thing in the morning?" he agreed calmly, surprising her.

"No, I can't. Mac and I are going to Lubbock."

He didn't remain calm. "You and Mac? Why are you going to Lubbock with Mac?" He grabbed her shoulders, as if to keep her from running away.

"Is that any of your business?"

She watched in fascination as he regrouped.

"Uh, I meant to say, I could take you to Lubbock, if you need something."

"I appreciate the offer, but Mac is already going, so there's no need to disrupt your day." She smiled sweetly at him and picked up her purse from the chair where she'd left it. "Are you ready to go?"

"Sure," he agreed and followed her out, waiting as she locked the door. "Uh, if it's a prescription you need filled, we have a drugstore here in town."

"No, it's not." She knew she should tell him why

she was going into Lubbock, but it was fun watching him try to figure out what was going on.

"Our grocery store has pretty much anything you need."

"I'm sure it does."

"Damn it, Alex, why are you going to Lubbock?"

She grinned. He'd lasted longer than she'd expected. "I'm going to Lubbock to buy a car."

THE ENTIRE TIME they grocery shopped, Tuck worried over Alex's announcement. He'd suggested he fly back to Dallas and drive her car to Cactus, but she'd refused his offer.

So she was going to Lubbock with Mac. Mac would get to help her choose a car. Mac would spend at least half a day with her. Mac would—

"Where's Mac going to take you?"

She looked up from the jar of peanut butter she'd been studying. "Didn't I tell you? To Lubbock."

"I mean, what dealership? Does he know someone he's recommended?"

"No. I'll decide when I get there."

Tuck frowned. "What kind of car?"

"I thought maybe a station wagon, or a sport utility vehicle."

"You mean you haven't even decided what kind of car? You'll never get around to buying one even if Mac escorts you."

"He's not going to escort me. He'll drop me off someplace. He has business to take care of."

Tuck's eyes widened. "You mean, you're going

"They treated me like family."

"And you're objecting?"

"Of course not!" she protested. "I loved it. But I didn't want them to have expectations that...that I can't fulfill."

"I told them you refused to marry me."

"Then why were they so nice to me?"

"Because they don't expect me to give up."

She stared at him as he calmly continued to drive. "Tuck, we live three hundred miles apart. We hardly know each other." She swallowed before she added, "I just don't see how things are going to work out."

"I believe they will. And in the meantime, we can spend time together. We already know we're sexually compatible."

"*You* know that. I don't."

"I'm willing to prove it anytime you want," he assured her with a sexy grin. "Though, I'd think the kisses we've shared would be enough to tell you there's a spark between us that might set off a forest fire."

She thought so, too. But she didn't want to tell him that.

AFTER HE GOT HOME, Tuck called Mac.

"Hi, Tuck. I tried to find you earlier, but I kept missing you."

"Is there a problem?" he asked, frowning.

"No, not at all. I wanted your opinion on the Wilson ranch. I've got a client who is interested in it, but I remembered you commenting on its condition a couple of months ago."

Tuck gave his opinion, not a favorable one. Then he brought up the subject he was interested in. "I hear you're taking Alex into Lubbock tomorrow."

"Yeah, she asked for a ride."

"Mind if I come along?" He'd tried to keep his voice casual, but Mac must've heard something.

"Jealous?"

With a sigh, Tuck gave an honest response. "Hell, yes, I'm jealous."

Mac chuckled. "I'd warn you against marriage if I didn't think you've already gone over the edge. Of course you can come with us. Does Alex know?"

"Nope. She'd tell me to stay home, so I thought I'd surprise her."

"Good plan. How did the trip to Dallas go?"

"Fine. Except for Chad Lowery."

"Is that the guy claiming to be the father?"

"Yeah. He's an attorney in her office. And a creep," Tuck added. "Alex thinks he's out for money. He's threatened to sue for custody of the baby…and child support, of course."

Mac whistled through his teeth. "Sounds like a lowlife. Does Alex have a lot of money?"

"According to Parker she does."

"The sooner you can prove this baby is yours, the better off things will be."

"Yeah. Or the sooner Alex gets her memory back. She's already remembering a few things." Tuck hesitated, then asked, "When you're driving into Lubbock, ask her about the law office she works for, will you?"

"Sure. What am I fishing for?"

"I'm not sure. Bill thinks there's something at the

office that's bothering her. Other than Lowery. He thinks she became a lawyer to please her father. Now that he's gone, she's not liking it. According to Bill."

"Has he got anything to back up his opinion?" Mac said, his voice serious.

"Nope. He says it's speculation on his part, but Alex tenses up when she goes into the office."

"Lowery—"

"Even when he's not there."

"It's understandable," Mac said. "I lost a lot of my enthusiasm about the legal profession while I worked in Dallas."

"Why? What happened?" Tuck had never questioned his friend's return to Cactus. Mac's divorce had been reason enough for his coming home.

"There's a lot of politicking in a law office. And a lot of pressure to bring in clients."

"I don't think that would be a factor. Alex owns half of her firm. She inherited it from her father."

"Her father? You don't mean she's Douglas Logan's daughter?" Mac asked, his voice rising.

"Yeah. Bill says he was well-known."

"Well, I guess. You've got yourself a very wealthy young woman. I read about his estate after his death, but I didn't connect it with Alex."

"So, do you think Bill's theory is right?"

"Hard to tell. But I'll see what I can get out of her tomorrow. It might be easier to talk business if you aren't along with us," Mac suggested.

Tuck grinned. "Nice try to get her alone. I'll keep quiet tomorrow, but I won't stay home. Where Alex goes, I go."

Chapter Ten

Alex was ready when she heard a car pull up the next morning. She grabbed her bag and hurried out, locking the door before she turned.

It wasn't a huge surprise to discover Tuck standing beside Mac's car.

"What are you doing here?" she asked.

"I thought I'd offer my assistance in car shopping."

"Tuck, I can manage on my own," she assured him, exasperation in her voice. "I did manage to exist before I met you, you know."

"I won't interfere if you don't want me to," he promised, holding up one hand as if taking an oath. "I'll just keep you company."

She accepted his promise and passed him to get in the back seat.

"No, you sit up front with Mac. I'm tagging along. I'll take the back seat." He held the front door open for her.

"But your legs are longer. I can—"

"I want you to ride up front," he insisted.

Frowning, Alex slid into the front seat. She didn't

understand why she was there, but it didn't seem worth fighting about.

"Morning," Mac said, smiling.

"Good morning. I really appreciate the offer of a ride, Mac."

"No problem. I told you I was glad for the company." He looked into the rearview mirror as he backed out, smiling at his second passenger. "I didn't know I'd get two for the price of one, but I should've suspected."

Alex looked over her shoulder at a smiling Tuck. "Aren't your cows going to miss you?"

"Dad said he'd go out and check on things today. He misses being out there."

"But your mother prefers town?"

"Yeah," Tuck said, still smiling, "but they compromised. It's a popular thing in marriages that work."

Alex recognized his implication. "The distance isn't quite as far as from here to Dallas, of course."

"True, but I'd even go that far to keep my family together."

Mac spoke. "I think this conversation has hidden meanings."

Alex smiled at him, glad for his presence. She didn't want another intense argument with Tuck. "Mac, didn't you say earlier that you'd worked in Dallas?"

He assured her he had, naming a prestigious law firm.

"That's a pretty high-powered outfit. Why'd you decide to come back to Cactus?"

She noted that Mac exchanged a look with Tuck in the mirror before he answered.

"I had a painful divorce, which was the main reason. But I was also tired of the politicking, the pressure to bring in clients. The backstabbing and jealousy. It seemed a far cry from the idealistic vision I had in law school about representing the downtrodden."

Dizziness passed through Alex's head as she listened to his words. It was almost as if he'd described her feelings.

"Alex? Are you okay?" Tuck asked urgently.

"Yes, of course. Why do you ask?"

"You turned pale suddenly. Do you need to lie down?"

"No, Tuck, I'm fine. I just—Mac said some things that I've felt." Things that she'd experienced. Because of her father's prominence, she was contacted by a lot of companies. They always wanted an "I'll scratch your back, you scratch mine" deal. Or they wanted her to bend the laws to protect them from their own behavior.

The case in Washington, D.C., had been particularly disturbing. Wilburt Denning, her client had—

"I remembered!"

Tuck leaned forward to touch her shoulder. "What did you remember?"

"The case I was working on in D.C.! I was experiencing a lot of what you talked about, Mac."

"Nothing else?" Tuck asked urgently. "Nothing personal?"

Alex took a minute to examine her thoughts, but

it was as if a curtain had fallen. "No, I'm sorry, Tuck, nothing personal." Tension rose in her.

"Don't worry about it," Mac said easily, again exchanging a look with Tuck. "Everything will come back gradually."

She sent him a smile of thanks before daring to turn to Tuck.

He looked angry and disappointed until he realized she was watching him. Immediately he put on a smile. "Mac's right. It's encouraging to see part of your memory return."

She wasn't fooled. "I'm really trying, Tuck. I don't know why—"

"Trying's probably the worst thing you can do, sweetheart. The doc said for you to relax."

"I know, but life would be a lot simpler if I could remember what happened." At least she thought it would be. If she knew whose baby she carried, though, Tuck would expect a decision about their future. Was that why she couldn't remember? Was she fearful of making that decision?

"Life is simple now," Tuck assured her. "You're going to relax in Cactus. Your biggest problem will be choosing my wallpaper."

"You're really going to have your kitchen redone?" Mac asked, changing the subject. Alex was grateful.

"Yeah. Now that Alex has promised to help me choose everything, I'd be crazy not to."

"You going to hire a housekeeper?" Mac asked.

"I think so." He paused, then said, "Should I ever marry, I don't want my wife to wear herself out with cooking and cleaning *and* raising the kids.

She might even have a career that would take some of her time."

Alex turned to stare at Tuck. "Did you have anyone in particular in mind?"

He gave her a wry look. "You know I do, sweetheart. But I don't want to put any pressure on you."

Right. No pressure at all.

TUCK KEPT his word.

At the three car dealers Alex decided to visit, he remained in the background, watching, saying nothing to interfere with her business. He'd made up his mind to follow that example last night.

After all, whether she got the best deal didn't matter. But learning to trust him was important.

Mac had loaned them his car while he took a deposition. They agreed to meet him for lunch at one o'clock.

"It's twelve-thirty," Tuck murmured in Alex's ear as she looked over a Chevrolet Blazer. "We need to meet Mac in half an hour."

"Right." She turned to the hovering salesman. "I'll take this one."

The man had tried to talk to Tuck, rather than Alex, at first. When he got no response from Tuck, he finally talked to Alex. Now he stared at her. "You'll take it?"

"Yes."

"This very car?"

"Yes, is there a problem?"

"No, not at all. We'll go back inside and discuss, uh, the price." He turned to walk to the showroom, but when he realized Alex wasn't following, he stopped. "Uh—"

"I don't want to make this complicated. I'll pay a thousand less than the listed price. I want it ready to go by two o'clock. Here's my banker's card. Call him and he'll wire the money."

Tuck smiled in appreciation. Here was the Alex he knew and loved. She went straight to the heart of what she wanted. The salesman still seemed to be in shock. For the first time, Tuck stepped forward. "We're on our way to lunch. Any questions?"

"Uh, no." The man continued to stare at Alex, as if he'd never seen a woman who could make a decision.

"Uh, we haven't discussed colors. Don't you want to talk about colors?"

Alex raised her eyebrows. "Were you planning on painting this vehicle?"

"No, but...but ladies like to talk about colors."

Alex's face grew stern. "Please listen carefully. I want this very vehicle. This *green* vehicle—and I want it ready by two o'clock. Can you do that?"

"Yes, ma'am. Sorry. Most people, uh, take more time to make their decision. You want this vehicle ready at two o'clock. You'll pay one thousand less than the list price, and I'm to call your banker."

His concentration earned a smile from Alex. "Exactly. Thank you very much."

"Thank you!" he said as Alex took Tuck's hand and started toward Mac's car. She waved over her shoulder.

"Are we going to be late?" she asked.

"Nope. Even if we were, Mac would forgive you."

"I know, but he was so nice to loan us his car, I don't want to keep him waiting."

Tuck's grin widened. She was some woman. He lifted her hand to his lips, surprising her.

"What are you doing?"

"I'm celebrating my good fortune."

She stopped and stared at him. "What do you mean?"

"I mean, you are a remarkable woman."

"Because I can buy a car?"

"Yeah, because you can buy a car." And because she knew her own mind. He wanted to care for her, to keep her safe. But he didn't want a woman who would cling. Alex was her own woman, which meant he'd have to fight to do anything for her.

"You're being ridiculous. Buying a car when you have plenty of money shouldn't be a big ordeal. If I were struggling because I had kids and no job and a husband who's a bum, then buying a car would be miraculous."

"Sweetheart, you'd manage. I have faith in you." His grin widened as she threw him an exasperated look before reaching for the passenger door of Mac's car.

Tuck slid behind the wheel. "What do you want for lunch?"

OVER LUNCH, Alex asked Mac questions about his law practice. She discovered he charged those who could afford his help and he did pro bono work for those who couldn't.

"I like that," she murmured. "I don't think my father ever helped anyone unless they were well-endowed."

Tuck took her hand. "Maybe you didn't know all his clients."

She recognized his desire to protect her, even from her memories of her father. "It's okay, Tuck. I realized what my father was like several years ago."

The sympathy on his face touched her.

"I'm sorry, sweetheart. That must be tough. My dad—well, he's a good guy."

"My mother was a good parent. I wish I'd told her how much she meant to me before she died. I know I told her I loved her, but...but I was in shock."

Mac cleared his throat. "I would imagine your mother knew she'd done a good job. Most people know when they do."

"Yes, I guess so. I don't think she had much joy in her life," Alex said, thinking about her childhood.

"Hey! You're remembering again," Tuck said, a big grin on his face.

Alex's eyes widened. "You're right. I remember my childhood, my parents. I even remember when I realized Dad wasn't...wasn't always a nice man." Tears gathered in her eyes and she blinked hard to keep them from falling.

Tuck slid a hand around her neck and pulled her close. Then his lips closed over hers. She wanted to protest his behaving like that in public, but she got too swept up in the feelings his lips evoked.

He released her without warning. "Finish your lunch. You don't want to keep Ed waiting."

"Who's Ed?" Mac asked.

"A car salesman who is probably still in shock," Tuck said with a big smile. He gave a humorous rendering of their car shopping to Mac.

Alex appreciated the time he gave her to recover. She knew he was sexy, intelligent and strong. But she'd never realized he was sensitive. No wonder she'd fallen for him.

She frowned. Was that a memory? Or had she fallen in love with Tuck since she'd come back to Cactus? She didn't know. She wasn't sure she could trust the feelings she had now.

She was so confused.

TUCK SAT SIDEWAYS in the passenger seat, watching how competently Alex handled the SUV. "What are you going to do with your Mercedes?"

"Sell it."

"Why? It's a nice car."

"I don't need a Mercedes here."

She answered in a distracted manner as she passed a slow truck on the road.

"So you're staying?" He fought back his excitement as he waited for her answer.

"What? Why would you say that?"

"You said you'd sell your Mercedes because you don't need it here in Cactus. That's what made me think you'd decided to stay."

She shot him an exasperated look. "I don't know what I'm going to do, Tuck. I told you that."

"Ah. I guess I forgot."

"Don't try to trick me," she said, firming her soft lips. "I know you're not being honest."

He laid his hand across his heart and widened his eyes in mock innocence. "Me? Not be honest? Why, ma'am, you do me wrong. A cowboy is always honest."

"A cowboy is full of it," she returned, but he was glad to see a smile on her beautiful face.

"Whatever you say, ma'am," he drawled. "A cowboy never disagrees with a beautiful woman."

"Then I must've been really ugly the first time you—" She broke off, staring at him in shock.

He grabbed the wheel. "Hey! Stay on your side, or you're going to have to buy another car."

She swallowed, turning her gaze back to the road.

"Are you all right?" Tuck asked, leaning forward to look at her face.

"Yes...yes, I'm fine."

Her voice sounded shaky. "I think you'd better take a nap when we get back to Cactus. You got up early this morning."

"Yes, I'll take a nap."

"Sure you don't want me to reschedule our appointment with Ralph?" he asked, worried about her. She still looked too pale. "It will mean another early morning tomorrow."

"No. No, I don't want you to reschedule. I'll make it, especially if I take a nap this afternoon."

"I left my truck at Mac's office, so you won't have to drive me home. And I drew a map for tomorrow morning." He'd tried to think of everything. He wanted to be sure she made the meeting in the morning. After all, he was redoing his kitchen for her.

They reached the outskirts of Cactus. Jessica's condo was only a couple of blocks from the town square. Alex stopped the Blazer outside of Mac's office on the square.

"Do you want me to go with you to the condo? I can walk back to my truck afterward."

"No, of course not. I'll be fine."

He continued to stare at her. Something didn't seem right. But the need to straighten the Blazer up, to pull back into their lane, had distracted him from whatever had happened.

If he could only remember what they'd been talking about. Something about being honest.

"Are you sure?" he asked again.

"I'm sure. Thank you for coming with me."

"My pleasure."

He pulled her close and kissed her. Until he felt the vehicle moving. "Alex!" he called.

She slammed her foot down on the brake only inches from a car parked at the curb. "Oh, dear," she said, panting, fanning herself with her hand. "I—I'd better get home and take my nap. 'Bye, Tuck."

"'Bye, sweetheart. Be careful."

"Yes, I will."

SHE WORKED to control herself until she had the Blazer safely in the condo driveway. After killing the motor, she leaned back against the seat and took a deep breath.

She'd remembered something more.

And this time it was personal.

She'd remembered Tuck teasing her, trying to convince her to have sex with him. He'd said he wanted to make love with her. And after the kisses they'd shared, she'd been grateful she'd managed to say no. She didn't move that quickly. Not with any man.

At least, she didn't think she did.

But she didn't know what her answer had been. That stupid curtain fell as soon as she tried to figure out what had happened.

Wearily, she dragged herself from the car and into the condo. Dropping her bag on the floor, she went up the stairs and headed for her bedroom. Falling across the bed, she closed her eyes.

She couldn't face any more today.

TUCK DIDN'T GO straight home. As he drove slowly in the direction of his ranch, he kept thinking about what had occurred on the road. Suddenly he made a U-turn in the middle of the road and headed back to his parents' house.

Every time Alex remembered something, it was because there was an echo of the past, a similarity to a memory. One of the best memories he had was of the barbecue they'd had for Jessica. He'd made sure Alex was invited.

When she'd showed up, he'd cut her out from the herd. He didn't want to share her with anyone. She'd knocked him off his feet the first time he'd met her and he hadn't been able to get her out of his mind. They had retired to the barn and a pile of hay.

She wouldn't let him recreate their lovemaking.

That thought brought a reaction that didn't surprise him. He could get hard just hearing her voice. But maybe he could bring back memories another way.

He stopped at his parents' house, charging in, calling out to his mother as he entered.

"Is the house on fire?" Ruth demanded as he rushed into the kitchen.

"No, of course not. But I needed to talk to you."

"Well, I'm here, boy. What do you need?"

"It's about Alex."

"Is she all right? She isn't sick, is she?"

"I don't think so. She's taking a nap. At least, she promised—that doesn't matter."

"I don't know, Tuck. For a healthy young woman, she sure does sleep a lot. Maybe you should take her to see Doc."

He frowned. "Yeah, I will, Mom. But it's okay. The doctor in Dallas said she should get a lot of rest. And it's working!"

"What's working? She's getting a lot of rest?"

"Yeah, and relaxing. And remembering."

"She remembers? She's going to marry you?" Ruth put down the spoon she was using to stir something, Tuck didn't know what, and came to kiss him on both cheeks.

"No, Mom. Not yet. She doesn't remember everything."

"And she won't tell you that she'll marry you until she remembers everything? I don't see why—"

"Mom! You're distracting me."

"Well, sorry, young man. I'm sure I didn't mean—" She backed away, her eyebrows raised.

Tuck immediately knew he'd hurt her feelings.

"Sorry, Mom. Look, I stopped here because I want you to help me."

"Help you do what?"

"Help me bring Alex's memory back."

Chapter Eleven

''Well, of course I'll help. That means you and Alex
will get married, doesn't it? I mean, that's what
you're waiting for.'' Ruth beamed. ''And since the
others are too busy making money to make babies,
I could still win!''

''Mom!'' Tuck protested. ''We're talking about
my life, my happiness, here. Not some stupid bet!''

His mother tried to look contrite, but the smile
remained in place. ''Of course, dear. I wouldn't
want you to marry Alex unless I thought it would
make you happy. You do love her, don't you?''

''Yeah. But that doesn't solve all our problems.''

''What problems?'' Ruth asked anxiously.

Tuck almost let the cat out of the bag. He caught
himself just as he was about to mention the baby.
And the daddy. ''Uh, whether Alex would be willing
to live here. I'm not sure I can live in Dallas. What
would I do with myself?''

''But she seems to like it here.''

''Temporarily.'' He ran a hand through his hair
and paced the kitchen. ''I don't know what will hap-

pen, Mom. I want her—but we have things between us, things that have to be settled.''

But he couldn't ask those hard questions until she'd recovered. He couldn't demand to know why she hadn't told him about the baby, when she didn't even know, right now, if it was his baby. He couldn't ask her what was bothering her, making her unhappy, with her work.

He couldn't ask anything yet.

"What do you want me to do?" Ruth asked, interrupting his dark thoughts…and fears.

He sighed. "Give a barbecue."

Ruth stared at him as if he was crazy. "Give a barbecue?"

"Yeah. I want to remind her of the barbecue we gave for Jessica. I think it will trigger some memories of that party."

"But…but why would that help? A barbecue?"

He could feel his face heat up but he gave her the answer to her question. "We, uh, didn't stay with the crowd all evening."

"Tuck! You didn't— Never mind." Ruth looked away. "Some things a mother just doesn't want to know."

"But you'll help me?"

"Yes, of course. And I'll get Mabel, Edith and Florence to help, too, just like before."

"And Jessica. She used her special sauce on the steaks."

"We'll have to get her to help. She won't give anyone that recipe," Ruth said. "We've tried."

"I don't think she can, by contract, Mom," he said, distracted as he tried to remember all the details of that evening almost five months ago. "Do you remember who was invited?"

"Everyone in town," Ruth returned immediately. "Even if they weren't invited, they showed up. And Ralph and his band played. We strung lights around the deck and—"

"I'll talk to Ralph in the morning when he comes to discuss the new kitchen. When can we have it?"

"Saturday night, I suppose. It was a Saturday night last time." Ruth tapped one finger against her lips. "I think we had baked potatoes, and we all baked pies." She turned and walked toward the door.

"Where are you going, Mom?" Tuck asked.

She blinked at him, as if surprised by his question. "Why, I'm going to make a list and call my friends. Isn't that what you want me to do?"

He stepped to her side and kissed her cheek. "Yeah, Mom, that's what I want. And thanks. You're the best."

ALEX DIDN'T WANT to get out of bed the next morning, but she'd promised Tuck she'd be at his house at eight. And she didn't want to disappoint him.

Was it because she loved him? Or because she wanted to fit in. She didn't know, but it was enough to make her get out of bed and dress.

When she arrived at Tuck's ranch, the map he'd drawn firmly clasped in her hand, she stared at the ranch house, seeking some memory.

But there was nothing.

With a sigh, she slid from behind the wheel of her new Blazer and walked to the front door. Tuck must've been watching for her because he opened the front door almost before she knocked.

"Morning," he said, his voice husky.

She gave a quick smile, waiting for him to move back, but he didn't. Instead he pulled her against him, the heat from his body encircling her, and lowered his lips to hers.

Her body shook off the drowsy state she hadn't been able to dispel and revved up, desire filling her. The man was too potent. She backed out of his hold, trying to catch her breath. "I hope Mr. Ralph isn't here yet," she whispered.

"Not 'mister.' Just Ralph. He's in the kitchen," Tuck told her, grinning as he reached for her hand and tugged her inside.

This time when she entered the kitchen she looked at it critically. The stove and refrigerator had certainly been made before she was born and the big sink had lost chips of enamel. The floor was uneven and worn.

"I see why you want to redo it," she said.

Tuck looked surprised. "It's not so bad."

An older man, who looked vaguely familiar, stood, a grin on his face. "For almost a hundred years old, it's not bad. Howdy, ma'am."

"Hello. Is it really that old?"

"Well, now, I reckon Tuck's grandparents built the house in the twenties, so maybe I stretched the truth a little. Good to see you again, Ms. Logan."

Alex took a step back. "I'm sorry, I don't remember."

"No problem. Tuck says you're gonna help figure out what to do about this here kitchen."

The man's easy acceptance relaxed Alex somewhat. Tuck's warm hand on her shoulder brought the tension back.

"Sit down at the table. I put water on for your herbal tea. I'll fix you a cup. Did you eat breakfast?"

"Not really. I didn't get up early enough." She smiled apologetically at Ralph. "I'm not an early riser by nature."

"No problem." He sat down at the kitchen table and shifted several large books.

Deciding those words were his response to just about everything, Alex was happy to join him. She was even more pleased when Tuck slid a plate with toast on it in front of her.

"Thank you," she said with a smile, and immediately sank her teeth into the crisp bread. "Just what I needed."

"Ralph, you want anything to eat?" Tuck asked.

"Nope. Just keep the coffee coming hot and black. Now, look here, Ms. Logan, Here are some pictures of kitchens I've done."

For the next half hour, Alex was amazed at how much she enjoyed herself. She'd never redone anything. Her family home had been elegantly appointed and she'd never dared move anything. When she sold it and bought her condo, again everything had been completed before she moved in.

"Will Tuck be able to use the kitchen while you're working on it?" she asked at one point.

"Prob'ly not, but don't matter. He don't cook much anyway." Ralph opened another book. "Here's some new things we could do."

He showed Alex the newest innovations and decor, surprising her with his knowledge. But she noticed he only showed her. Tuck sat beside her but showed little or no interest in what was going on.

"Tuck? Don't you want any say about your kitchen? You're not even paying attention," she complained after a few minutes.

"Nope. It doesn't matter much to me. I trust your taste. But I need the kitchen updated before I hire a housekeeper. Mom said any self-respecting woman would refuse to work in here."

"Why didn't your mother update it?"

He grinned. "She moved in here as a young bride and got used to it before they discovered oil. I guess she didn't think much about it."

"Oh."

"Once they moved into their new house, and she discovered all those conveniences, she said I should update, but, as Ralph said, I don't cook much. I've got a cook in the bunkhouse. I eat with my men."

"Well, once you hire a housekeeper, all that will change, so it should be something you like," she insisted, feeling a little uneasy about making all the decisions without any input from him.

"Once you've made a decision, you can run it by me, but as long as you don't decorate in tiger stripes, I'll probably agree." He smiled as if he had no concerns at all.

Shrugging her shoulders, she began discussing her choices with Ralph. If Tuck wasn't going to make any decisions, then she would.

A few minutes later she said, "I don't know,

Ralph. I like this countertop in the picture, but I'm not sure how it will look in real life."

"I've got a sample of it in my truck. I'll go get it." The older man hurried out the back door before Alex could protest.

"What do you think of it?" she asked Tuck.

"Hmm?" he answered, looking at her. "Think of what?"

"The countertop, Tuck."

"I think I'm more interested in you," he assured her. Before she knew what was happening, he'd reached over and lifted her from her chair to his lap. His lips immediately sealed off any protest she might've made, if she had a single coherent thought. But the taste of him, all male and hungry need, washed any protest from her head.

He finally lifted his mouth, only to bury his face in her hair, his lips tracing her neck.

"Tuck, Ralph will be back in a minute," she whispered even as she pushed closer to his strong frame.

"Yeah," he agreed, but continued his tasting of her soft skin. "Maybe next we'll work on a bedroom."

"Tuck! We can't—"

"Why not? We already did, and the proof is right here," he pointed out, rubbing his hand over her stomach.

"The baby isn't proof of anything," she protested, moving back from his embrace, regretful that he'd reminded her of her difficulties.

"*Our* baby is proof that we belong together," Tuck insisted.

And that was the crux of the matter. A baby wasn't a reason for a marriage. She wanted Tuck to love her, to want her, for herself alone. Until she got back her memory—

"You folks having a baby?" Ralph asked in surprise from the back door.

RUTH MADE HER PHONE CALLS. She asked each of her friends to help her with the barbecue Saturday night, even though she explained that she hoped to win the contest because of that barbecue. As she'd expected, all three of them immediately offered to help.

"Of course I'll help you," Mabel said. "Though I still think Cal and Jessica will win. You know, I saw her the other day in silhouette, and I believe she's putting on weight. Jessica's never had a weight problem."

"I wish I could say the same for Alex. She looks a little more fragile than ever. Tuck says she has to rest all the time. Doctor's orders so she'll get her memory back," Ruth explained with a sigh. "But gettin' them married is a step in the right direction."

"You bet. That would make three down and only one to go. We could all concentrate on Mac if Tuck marries."

"Poor Florence," Ruth said, sympathy in her voice. Ruth was already counting herself in the successful group with Mabel and Edith. She hoped she wasn't jumping the gun.

Edith was just as supportive. "I'm so glad to be able to help. I like Alex. I hope she stays here."

"Me, too. I'd die if I finally got a grandbaby and they took it to Dallas." Ruth shuddered.

"Yeah, they have crime in those big cities," Edith agreed, then added with satisfaction, "Melanie likes it in Cactus."

Even though she sounded depressed, Florence, also, was eager to help. "I think I baked about six apple pies. Will we need more this time?"

"Don't think so. It'll be about the same size party as last time. Tuck hopes it'll help Alex remember. Then they can marry."

"They haven't spent a lot of time together, have they? Are you sure they'll be ready for marriage?"

Ruth tried to hide her irritation at Florence raining on her parade. "I think so. You can tell when they're together that they're in love."

"Then that's all that matters. What do I need to do besides bake pies?"

Ruth consulted her list.

"NO!" ALEX SHOUTED. She jumped from Tuck's lap as if she'd been shot out of a cannon.

"Yeah," Tuck said at the same time, squaring his jaw.

"No, we're not," Alex repeated. "We were…were talking about the *possibility* of having a baby if…if we married."

Ralph seemed unconcerned about their answers. "No puttin' the cart before the horse, eh?" He chuckled. "Good idea."

Then he returned to the subject of the kitchen. "Here's the countertop sample I was talking about,

Alex. It's small, but you can see how it looks in real life.''

Tuck ignored the talk about his future kitchen. He was tired of denying the existence of his child. Tired of being put off by the woman he intended to marry. He got up and crossed the room to the phone.

"Cal? It's Tuck. I think it's time."

His friend sounded surprised. "Time for what?"

"To let out the secret."

"Whoa! I can't make that decision. Jess would kill me. I think we'll have to defer to the ladies on this one, Tuck.''

"Easy for you to say. Your lady is cooperating.'' He stared across the room at Alex, his gaze caressing her glowing face.

He needed more. More time spent with her. More kisses. More than kisses. It was only Thursday. He couldn't wait until Saturday night.

Not that revealing the three pregnancies would actually settle the questions. But it meant he could stop lying.

"Hey," Cal said into the silence, "Mom called and said we're having another barbecue Saturday night. Maybe we could talk the ladies into making the big announcement then. What do you think?"

"Sounds good to me. I'm tired of all the pretence."

"How's Alex doing? I heard about her trip to Lubbock.''

Tuck leaned against the wall, continuing to stare at her. "She's doing fine. More and more like her old self. And she's beginning to remember things."

Cal paused before asking, "Why don't you sound happy about that?"

"Because I'm not sure what all was going on four months ago. She wasn't talking to me about her problems. Well, I guess we didn't talk much about anything, but—"

"Yeah," Cal said, the one word holding understanding and sympathy.

"Anyway, talk to Jess about Saturday night. I'll call Spence and Melanie tonight."

"Why don't we all meet at the Roundup and have dinner together? And we can include Mac. He'll act as a voice of reason."

"Let me check with Alex. Hang on." He covered the receiver with his hand. "Alex? Cal wants to know if we want to have dinner at the restaurant tonight with everyone."

"That would be nice," she agreed with a smile before turning back to Ralph to continue their discussion.

"She said okay," Tuck reported.

Cal chuckled. "Would you have believed, this time last year, how much we'd all be tied to the apron strings?"

"I'm not tied yet," Tuck assured him.

But Cal had the last laugh. "I know, but you want to be, don't you?" After laughing again, he said goodbye and hung up.

His friend was right. He wanted to be married to Alex, living here in Cactus, waiting for the arrival of their child.

Only a few things stood in the way. He didn't know for sure that the baby was his, Alex had refused his offer of marriage, and he didn't know if she'd agree to remain in Cactus even if she did agree to marry him.

But at least he knew what he wanted.

AFTER LUNCH, Alex insisted on returning to her condo. She thought she might need to rest if they were going out that night, and she believed Tuck needed to work.

He'd given up a lot of time to her in the past week. But she knew, from what he'd said and what she'd observed, that ranching took a lot of hard work. The day he'd escorted her around the ranch, he'd said he put in ten- or twelve-hour days in the summer, when the light lasted longer.

If she married him, she'd—

Alex came to a complete halt in the middle of the stairs. Another memory. He'd given her a tour of his ranch on that first Sunday afternoon, while Jessica went to see Cal about something.

She'd been enchanted with the crisp fall weather, the barn, the corrals, the animals. Tuck had said that cows weren't very bright, but she liked them. And the horses! She'd fallen in love with the horses. Tuck had promised to teach her to ride.

Instead, the next time they'd been together, he'd been distracted. And so had she. That was the barbecue. He'd led her into the dark barn and—

Yep, he could definitely be the father of her baby.

But what about Chad? Had she actually been sleeping with two men at once? Had she gone from Chad's arms to Tuck's?

The thought of that behavior sickened her.

Unable to shake her thoughts, or to remember any more, she turned around and headed back down the stairs. Maybe now was a good time to visit Mac's office.

After parking in front of the office of Maxwell Gibbons, Attorney-at-law, lettered in gold on the picture window, Alex opened the door and entered into a charming reception area. A gray-haired lady, busy at the computer, looked up.

"Good afternoon. May I help you?"

Alex smiled. The woman reeked with efficiency. "I was hoping to see Mac. Is he busy?"

"I'll check. May I tell him who's calling?"

"Alexandra Logan."

The woman showed no recognition and excused herself gracefully.

Alex sat in the nearest navy leather chair. Mac hadn't skimped on the decorating, she decided.

Before she could settle in, the door opened and Mac preceded his secretary into the room. "Alex! You came. Come on in to my office. Oh, let me introduce Vera. She's the best secretary any man could have."

"Hello," Alex said, smiling.

The woman's formality had disappeared. "Hello. Welcome to Cactus. I understand you practice law in Dallas?"

"I did. But I'm visiting in Cactus now."

After a nod, Vera returned to work and Alex followed Mac. The door from the reception area led to a small hall with four doors. Curious, she peeked into the rooms. One was a library and storeroom. Another the bathroom. The third was empty and the fourth, the largest of the rooms, was Mac's office, as tastefully decorated as his reception area.

"Very nice. Your office would fit right in with any firm in Dallas," she assured him as she sat down.

"Thanks. Actually, it's nicer than the office I had in Dallas. I was only a junior member of the firm, after all," he assured her with a grin. "I'm glad you came to see me. I was serious about needing some help."

"Research?" she asked.

"That. And maybe some lawyering, too." He leaned back in his chair behind the desk. "I didn't intend to work this hard when I opened shop. I don't ever get to take the day off to go fishing or riding anymore. Want to hang out your shingle in Cactus?" he asked, smiling again.

It hadn't been her intent. But his offer fit like a glove. A law office where she could do what she loved to do without all the stress. A place where she could help people. "You know," she said, a considering look on her face, "I think I'd like that."

Chapter Twelve

"You're not serious, are you?" Mac asked, surprise on his face.

"Weren't you? I thought you said you were."

Mac studied her and she held her breath for his reply.

"I'm serious about needing help," he said slowly, still staring at her as if seeking a clue for a puzzle. "But I didn't think you'd have any interest in— There's not much money in this kind of a practice."

"I don't have to worry about money. Do you?" She wasn't bragging. Long ago she'd dealt with any guilt she felt for having inherited a lot of money.

"No. What about your job in Dallas?"

Alex got up and paced across Mac's office. "I don't want to go back. I think...I think one of the reasons for my amnesia was stress from my job. I don't much like practicing law in a big city. I think I'm becoming too cynical."

"But you own part of the firm, don't you?"

"There's a buyout clause. I checked about six months ago, before I came here the first time. I've been thinking about calling it quits for a while."

Another memory. She didn't stop to point that out to Mac. "But I didn't know what I'd do with myself. I really love being a lawyer when I can help someone. I volunteered at a woman's shelter, offering legal advice for the women."

She turned around and sat back down to face Mac. "Would you be interested in taking on a partner?"

"I'd be delighted," he said with no hesitation, grinning at her. "Want me to draw up partnership papers?"

Alex leaned back in the wing chair, trying to consider everything. She hadn't expected things to move so fast, but it felt right.

"I want to, Mac. I really want to. Just thinking about joining you here gives me peace. I haven't had that in a long time."

Just as he leaned forward to speak, the phone rang. "Don't lose that thought," he said with a grin, and answered the phone. "Hello? Tuck! What a coincidence. I'm talking to Alex."

Before he could say anything else, Alex began frantically waving at him, shaking her head no, holding a finger to her lips. Fortunately, Mac seemed to get her message.

"We're comparing notes on working in Dallas. Yeah, she's fine."

Alex figured Tuck was calling to invite Mac to dinner. After a brief silence, Mac confirmed her speculation.

"Yeah, that would be great. At seven? See you then."

To Alex's surprise, he then handed the phone to her. "Tuck wants to talk to you."

She put the phone to her ear. "Hello?"

"I thought you were going to take a nap."

"I felt restless. Mac had invited me to see his office, so I came over here."

"I just don't want you to get too tired."

"I'm fine, Tuck," she said firmly. If she let him, he'd completely take over her life. She couldn't remember why that would be a bad thing, but she was sure it would be.

"All right. I'll pick you up a little before seven."

"I could drive myself."

"You could, but you won't," he said with a growl. "See you, sweetheart."

She handed the phone back to Mac.

"Now, where were we?" Mac asked, a teasing grin on his face.

"Mac, there's a problem."

"What's that?"

"I want— I really like it here in Cactus. But until I settle things with Tuck, I can't— It would be awkward to move here if Tuck and I don't remain friends."

Mac leaned back in his chair. "Do you think that's going to happen?"

She felt her cheeks flushing. So much for her reputed cool sophistication. "If the baby isn't Tuck's, I doubt that his offer of marriage will stand."

"Then you don't know Tuck very well."

"Maybe that's part of the problem. The attraction we both felt was so strong, we skipped a few steps along the way. And now I can't even remember what little time we had together.'' She twisted her hands together in her lap.

''Well, we can work out a partnership agreement but not execute it until other things have been settled,'' he suggested, watching her.

''I'd like that. Would you consider representing me with my law firm, negotiating the buyout?'' she asked.

''Sure, I'd be glad to, Alex, but you could handle that yourself,'' he reminded her.

She rubbed her stomach until she realized what she was doing and quickly laced her fingers. ''I don't think the stress would be good for me. The buyout should be fairly straightforward. I'll call my secretary and have her fax you the agreement.''

''Go ahead and call her. Here's our fax number. I'll go make sure the machine is on,'' he said before he slipped out of the office, giving her privacy.

Within half an hour, Mac had the papers in front of him. ''This should be a piece of cake, Alex. And you will be a very rich young woman. We'll get all the papers ready. Then, when you're ready, we can—''

''I'm ready. I'm not returning to the office, except to clean out my personal belongings. If I don't stay here, I'll find some other small town.''

''You're sure?''

''Would you go back?'' she asked softly.

The look he gave her made Alex feel she'd made a very good friend in Mac Gibbons. It wasn't the same feeling she had about Tuck. Not even close. But a nice one, even so.

''Nope. I'd never go back.''

"Neither will I."

He checked his watch. "It's four-thirty now. I'll get on this first thing in the morning," he said with a firm nod. Then he put the agreement on one side of his desk. "Now, how about doing something fun?"

"What?" she asked, surprised by his words.

"Why don't we go over to Melanie's shop and see if she has some good furnishings for your future office."

"But we're not sure—"

"I need to furnish that office anyway."

"Okay, but I have one request."

"What's that."

"I don't want you tell Tuck about our conversation. It has to remain a secret."

TUCK DIDN'T SADDLE UP that afternoon, as he'd originally planned. After Ralph and Alex had finished their discussions, they'd presented him with a plan for his new kitchen. While they'd been talking, he'd made sandwiches. After approving their decisions, he invited them to eat lunch.

He would've preferred that Ralph leave, letting Tuck have lunch with Alex alone. But Ralph was a working man, a friend. He couldn't send him off without a good meal.

Then he'd had to let Alex leave alone, so he could talk to Ralph about the barbecue. Fortunately, the man didn't think he and his band had any plans for Saturday night, so Tuck could mark that chore off the list.

After checking in with his mother, he called Melanie at her shop.

"Mel, I'm having some problems keeping the secret about the babies. Cal thought we should all meet tonight at the restaurant to talk about it."

"Tonight? I usually keep the store open until nine on Thursday nights, Tuck."

"Oh. Well, I guess we could drop by the store after dinner and tell you if we came up with any ideas. But I should tell you that we're going to have a barbecue Saturday night. Cal thought it might be a good time to make the announcement."

"A barbecue?" Melanie asked, sounding distracted.

"Yeah, like the one we had last October for Jessica. I want to surprise Alex. I'm hoping it will jog her memory."

"What a good idea. I'm glad you said it was a surprise, though, or I would've said something to her."

"Don't you think it will be better if it's a surprise?" Tuck was still undecided about that.

"Yes, I think you're right. You know, I think I'll close the store early tonight and come to dinner. We have a lot to discuss."

"Are you sure?"

"I never have a lot of customers at night anyway," she told him with a chuckle. "Wishful thinking on my part. I'll call Spence. What time should we come?"

"Seven. I'm going to call Mac, too. Cal said he could be the voice of reason."

"He always is. And maybe socializing with all us

pregnant women will make him want his own baby.''

''I kind of doubt it,'' Tuck said, trying to give a civil reply to something he believed would never happen. ''Don't forget, the barbecue is a surprise.''

''No, I won't. We'll see you at the restaurant.''

Then he called Mac, only to discover Alex was there instead of resting at the condo.

Disturbed, maybe even a little jealous, Tuck tried to do some office work for the next hour before he got ready to go to dinner. Mac was his friend. He knew Mac wouldn't try anything with Alex. But it was Alex he was worried about. She and Mac had so much in common.

He ended up ready a half hour early. Then he paced the floor until it was time to leave.

MELANIE WAS WAITING on an elderly lady who was considering the purchase of a beautiful teapot. She looked up as Alex and Mac stepped into her shop and her eyes widened with pleasure.

They stood quietly by as the customer made her purchase. After she'd left the store, Mac stepped forward. ''Good afternoon, Madam Owner. How's it going?''

''Okay. I may even make enough this month to pay my bills,'' she assured them with a big smile, unfazed by her slow start. ''Spence keeps saying it will pick up. He's so wonderful.''

''I think he's right. I've decided to furnish my second office. Alex has agreed to help me pick out the furniture. It'll save me a lot of money, not hiring an expensive decorator.''

Alex was relieved when Melanie didn't question Mac's concocted story. Melanie was too excited about making a sale.

"I have several desks," she said, leading them across the room. "I know which I would prefer, but it's the most expensive. I don't want to push you into anything."

Mac grinned at Alex. "You can tell she's one of those high-pressure salespeople. I don't know how we can handle her tactics."

Alex smiled back, relaxing again. Life in Cactus was wonderful. How she hoped she could stay, be a part of this friendship. Share her life with Tuck.

"What do you think?" Melanie asked.

Alex pulled her attention back to furniture. For the next half hour, she and Melanie dashed from one part of the store to another, pulling together an eclectic mix of furniture and decorations.

"Oh, it's going to look great," Alex said with a sigh when they'd finished. "Mac, did we spend too much?" she asked, suddenly realizing he was preparing to pay. She'd pay him back, of course, but she couldn't tell him that in front of Melanie.

But she wanted to. She wanted to tell all of them she would become a part of their lives. It was so tempting. But just thinking about what could happen if she and Tuck— It didn't bear thinking about.

Mac didn't seem to be bothered by the price of their choices. "Nope. I think you did a classy job. Maybe you should give up law and become a decorator."

"I don't think so, but I had fun."

Melanie looked up from the adding machine she

was using. "I had more than fun," she assured them with a grin. "Even with the discount, this is the best day I've ever had. Heck, this total is better than the best month I've had."

"You've only been open one month," Mac reminded her. "And what's this about a discount?"

"When someone buys as much as you, you get a discount," she told him hurriedly.

"I remember telling you I didn't charge my friends for legal services, and you set me straight in a hurry."

Melanie looked at Alex, and she stepped forward to see if she could help. "Consignment stores usually negotiate on prices."

"That's right," Melanie agreed.

"Then we'll negotiate," Mac agreed pleasantly. "You'll tack back on half the discount. That's a compromise. Otherwise, I'll go to Lubbock for my furniture."

"You wouldn't!" Melanie said with a gasp, her pretty face showing how devastating such an action would be.

Alex didn't think Mac would do such a horrible thing, but she thought his offer was fair. "As your attorney, Mel, I recommend you take his offer. Then you'll both be happy. And me, too. I love all the things we picked out."

Melanie agreed and they quickly settled up.

"We've got to hurry to get to the restaurant on time," Melanie added as she handed Mac his receipt. She'd promised to have the men she hired deliver the furniture tomorrow.

Alex checked her watch. "Oh, no! Tuck is picking me up in a few minutes. I've got to run!'' She dashed out of the store, all the time thinking about what a wonderful day she'd had.

TUCK HAD had another idea.

While he'd paced, waiting to go pick up Alex, it had occurred to him that even if the baby was his, and she agreed to marry him, they might not have settled all their problems.

Alex wouldn't want to be a housewife.

And there was no reason why she should. She seemed to be a very good lawyer. It would be a waste of her talents to stop being an attorney.

So he planned to help her.

All of that flew out of his mind when she opened the door to the condo. Instead of hurrying her to the restaurant so they wouldn't be late, he gently pushed her back inside and closed the door behind them.

''Tuck, what are you—''

She didn't have to ask, then. As his lips took hers, his arms encircled her, his hands caressed her body, she slid her arms around his neck and cooperated to the fullest.

So much so that Tuck was ready to head for the stairs and the waiting bed. When he picked her up, however, her cooperation ended.

''Tuck, what are you doing? We're expected at the restaurant.'' Her voice was husky but firm.

''Damn! Steak's not what I'm hungry for.''

She nibbled on her bottom lip and he thought he'd die if he didn't kiss her again. Standing her down, his lips took hers again.

When he lifted his head, they were both breathing heavily.

"We...we'd better go," she whispered.

"Are you sure?"

Her hands still rested on his chest, and she fingered the collar of his leather jacket. "I'm sure."

The ride to the restaurant was too short for him to gather his thoughts. They were all centered on Alex and how she felt in his arms.

When they reached the restaurant and their friends, Tuck's earlier idea came back to him, but he would have to wait for an opportunity to talk to Mac alone.

Once they were all seated and had placed their orders, Tuck realized he'd forgotten to tell Cal the barbecue was a secret.

"A barbecue?" Alex repeated after Cal's suggestion that they announce the existence of the babies on Saturday night. "Why are you having a barbecue?"

"Tuck said—" Cal began, only to be cut off by Tuck.

"That we wanted to celebrate your return. Barbecues are fun. You'll like it." Damn, he must be getting old, or confused. Or his hormones were blocking his thought processes. Cal had suggested they announce the babies at the barbecue. But he'd thought he could keep it a secret from Alex. He was crazy.

"I'm sure I will," Alex agreed.

"You sure liked the last one," Jessica said with a grin.

Tuck swallowed his groan. Well, so much for his plan.

"When was that?" Alex asked.

As everyone filled in Alex's memory, Tuck watched her closely, wondering if she'd recall anything about that other night. But in spite of her questions, she showed no signs of remembering.

When there was a pause in the conversation, he brought up the reason for their dinner again. "What about announcing the babies that night? Anyone have a problem with that?"

"I don't," Mac said. "I think Aunt Florence will feel better when she knows the game is over. Right now, she's still fretting about me not marrying. If it doesn't end soon, I think both of us will go crazy."

"I agree it's probably time," Melanie agreed with a sigh. "But what about you and Alex? I mean, do you want to reveal your pregnancy?" she asked, looking at Alex.

Tuck watched as Alex straightened her shoulders, then said quietly, "I'm not ashamed of my baby."

"Oh, no! I didn't mean— I meant that until you know who the father is— Oh, Alex, I said the wrong thing." Melanie looked as if she was about to cry. Spence slid his arm around her and hugged her close.

"I wasn't offended," Alex hurriedly assured her. "Really, I know what you meant," she added.

Tuck smiled at her, proud of her sympathetic response.

"Of course you did," Jessica agreed. "Come on, Melanie, we all know you wouldn't say anything mean."

Once Melanie was reassured, the question rose for the third time. Spence said, "So, are we agreed?"

Everyone nodded. Then Jessica brought up another point. "Do we tell our parents beforehand or in front of everyone?"

Spence grinned. "I'd like to tell them in front of everyone. You know, share the humor. But I'm afraid my mother would disown us."

"That would be cruel," Melanie said. "Especially since we're all four months pregnant. They still won't know who will win the contest."

"True," Mac agreed. "But Aunt Florence will know she can't win. At least that part of the race will be over."

"So we'll each tell our parents before the barbecue, including about the other babies?" Melanie asked.

"And I'll tell Aunt Florence," Mac added.

"Whew!" Cal said with a sigh. "I'm glad that's settled. I've been reluctant to spend any time with Mom and Dad, afraid I'd say the wrong thing. Dad asked me the other day if we were mad at them."

"You didn't tell me that," Jessica said with a frown.

"I didn't want to upset you, baby. You're not supposed to get stressed out."

"Which brings us back to Alex. You okay, sweetheart?" Tuck asked, his hand caressing her warm shoulder.

"Yes. I agree. It will be a relief to…to not hide anything."

Tuck noticed she shot a quick glance at Mac. That ridiculous jealousy flared again.

"True. It's hard to keep secrets," Mac said with a smile that made Tuck just a little suspicious. Until Alex turned to look at him, and he was instantly reminded of their earlier kisses.

He wanted to kiss her again.

"Um, want to go home? Are you tired?" he asked, hoping to get her to himself.

"Tuck, they just brought our steaks," Jessica protested. "Alex is eating for two. You mustn't take her away before she can eat."

"Oh, yeah. I—I forgot." He turned his attention to his steak, hoping no one realized why he'd offered to take her away. But he figured all three of his friends knew what was on his mind.

Suddenly he remembered his earlier plan. "Uh, I need to excuse myself for a minute." He shot Mac a hard stare, hoping he'd take a hint.

Mac continued to eat his steak, ignoring Tuck.

"Mac."

His friend looked up. "Yeah, Tuck?"

"Want to come with me?"

"Where?" Mac asked, looking confused.

Tuck glared even harder.

"Oh, uh, yeah, I'll come with you."

Tuck knew Mac still didn't know where he was going. It was a sign of their friendship that he'd blindly agreed. Tuck stood and walked toward the rest rooms on the other side of the restaurant, hoping Mac was following.

When he went inside the facility, he leaned against the wall and waited for Mac.

"What's up, Tuck?" Mac asked at once. "Guys don't go to the bathroom in pairs, like ladies."

"They do if they want a private conversation," Tuck informed him, irritated with his remark.

"Oh. What do we need to be private about?"

"I have a plan, and I need your help."

"The barbecue? I'll do whatever you need. I think it's a good idea, by the way."

Distracted, Tuck said, "I got the idea from you. Talking about your problems with the legal profession is what made Alex remember how she felt. I thought by having parallel events, she might remember more."

"Good thinking." Mac turned to leave.

"Wait! That's not what I wanted to talk to you about."

Mac blinked in surprise. "Then why are we talking about it?"

"We're not— I mean, you— Never mind! I want you to do something for me. But you have to promise first."

"Promise what?"

"That you won't tell Alex my plan."

Chapter Thirteen

"What plan?" Mac asked, still looking confused.

"I want you to offer her a job. You know," Tuck continued as Mac stared at him, "you talked about needing help at the office."

After a pause that had Tuck wondering about Mac's willingness to cooperate, Mac said, "Yeah, and I mentioned that to Alex."

"I know, but I want you to offer her a real job."

"Why?"

Tuck began pacing in the small area. "I want her to feel that she won't be giving up too much if she stays here."

"You're afraid she'll miss Dallas?"

"She might. I mean, you and I prefer Cactus, but women like bright lights, a lot of action."

"Jessica and Melanie don't."

"They're different," Tuck said, his mind still on Alex.

"Look, Tuck, I—"

The door opened and Cal entered. "What's going on in here? Is everything all right?"

Tuck sighed. "Of course everything's all right. I just needed to talk to Mac privately."

"Well, excuse me," Cal said, offended.

"Hell, Cal, I didn't mean I didn't want you to hear," Tuck protested. "I meant Alex."

"There's a problem between Mac and Alex?" Cal turned to stare at Mac. "We just heard about your shopping trip."

"What shopping trip? You mean, for the car? I was there," Tuck assured Cal.

"No, the one this afternoon."

Tuck spun around to stare at Mac. "What's he talking about?"

Mac shoved his hands into his pockets and leaned against the wall. "This afternoon, Alex offered to help me pick out furniture for my second office. We went to Melanie's store and found what we needed."

Cal grinned. "Melanie was ecstatic."

"Perfect!" Tuck exclaimed, his mind still on his plans for Alex.

"What do you mean?" Cal asked, looking at first Tuck and then Mac.

"I want Mac to encourage Alex to work for him."

"Does she need the money?" Cal asked, frowning.

"Hardly," Mac said.

At the same time, Tuck said no.

"Then why—"

"So she'll be able to use her talents. I think she's a pretty good lawyer."

Mac corrected Tuck. "She's an excellent lawyer.

Don't let her pretty looks fool you. She's sharp as a tack.''

"Would she be willing to work for someone else?'' Cal asked.

Tuck frowned. He hadn't thought about that aspect. Would Mac be willing to take her on as an equal? He was trying to think of an inducement that would encourage Mac to do so, when the bathroom door opened.

Jerry Brockmeier, owner of the local drugstore and one-time employer of Melanie, stepped inside. "Oh, sorry, I didn't realize there'd be a line.'' Then he looked beyond the three men to see four vacant urinals.

"Go ahead, Jerry,'' Cal said, waving his hand. "We're, uh, talking.''

But none of them said a word as Jerry took care of business. When he slid past them and out the door, Tuck breathed a sigh of relief. "Now, where—''

The door opened again.

This time it was Spence. "Guys, what's going on? The ladies are getting worried.''

Cal looked at all his friends, then roared with laughter. "I think we'd better get back to the table before some nasty rumors start.''

Mac leaned toward Tuck. "Don't worry. I'll take care of it.''

Tuck had to be satisfied with those words because he couldn't continue the conversation at the table.

"I FEEL BAD about Mac's aunt,'' Melanie said when the three ladies were left at the table. "It seems sad that she's left out."

"Yeah, it is," Jessica agreed. "And Mac should marry. He's a great guy, but his first marriage has scared him off."

"Was she awful?" Alex asked.

"The worst," Jessica said. "Though I shouldn't say that. I only met her once. After their marriage, she came here once. And hated it."

"Cactus?" Alex asked, wondering what could have been wrong with the woman.

"Yep. She said we were much too provincial for her tastes," Jessica said, imitating the woman's snotty tones. "She pushed Mac for more money and more prestige. He didn't tell her about the oil and gas money he had. When her husband died, Florence had signed over her husband's shares to Mac."

"So she didn't know he was already wealthy?" Melanie asked. "How could he hide it?"

"He lived on his salary, which wasn't chicken feed. When he realized that Tiffany wasn't the sweet young woman he'd thought he married, he got out of the marriage."

"Did he lose much of his money?" Alex asked, knowing how divorces went.

"Some. But he didn't care. He said it was worth it to not be married to her anymore."

"I'm sorry," Alex murmured. Mac had been so kind to her today. It really would be a shame if he never married.

Jessica leaned forward and lowered her voice. "I think we should try to fix Mac up. There's got to be some lady who will entice him back into marriage. Then we'd have a foursome.''

Alex realized Jessica was taking her inclusion for granted. "If I'm here."

"Of course you'll be here. You and Tuck are perfect for each other."

"Jessica, I don't know. I can't remember much. I mean, some of it's coming back, but we didn't get to know each other as well as we should've. What if I make a mistake?"

"You sound like I did," Melanie said.

"What do you mean?"

"Spence and I... I got pregnant on Jessica's wedding day, but Spence and I hadn't dated. I didn't want to marry just because of the baby."

Alex let out a relieved sigh. "That's exactly how I feel."

"But, Alex," Jessica said, leaning forward again, "you can't doubt that Tuck loves you."

"Yes, I can. He wants me, that I can't doubt, but I don't know that he loves me. Something is bothering him."

"Well, the fact that the baby may be another man's could have something to do with it," Jessica returned, as if she were defending Tuck.

"I know, but—"

"Sorry, ladies, for being gone so long," Cal said, sliding into place beside Jessica.

Alex's gaze quickly flew to Tuck, who avoided looking at her as he sat down. She turned her gaze to Mac, who gave her a nod of reassurance.

Tuck scarcely spoke the rest of the dinner. Alex watched him, hoping she hid the hunger she felt to reach out and touch him. Both Jessica and Melanie had the right to hold their husbands' hands, to touch their arms, to even share a brief kiss.

Alex didn't.

But she could. If she allowed herself to become Tuck's lover, she could have that right. That thought took her breath away. She'd been fighting the attraction ever since she'd come to Cactus with Bill Parker. Immediately she'd felt Tuck's potency in every touch.

Why had she been fighting him so hard?

She had no answer.

When dinner was over, Jessica asked if anyone wanted to hear the band, but everyone seemed ready to go home. Alex told her friends good-night, even as her mind focused on Tuck, and their relationship.

Only Mac's whisper disrupted her thoughts. As he leaned over to kiss her cheek, he whispered, "Tuck suggested you go to work with me."

She stared at him, her eyes large. Mac leaned over again and whispered, "His idea. I said nothing."

"Hey," Tuck protested. "One kiss to a customer, Mac."

Mac grinned at his friend. "Now, Tuck, watch those jealous eyes. You know I'd never poach on your property even if I was shopping for a bride."

Everyone laughed, and Jessica added, "Maybe one day you will be."

"Don't make any such remarks around Aunt Florence," Mac pleaded. "Things are bad enough as it is."

"Maybe we'll help your aunt. What color of hair do you like?" Cal teased.

"Anything as long as it's not blond," Mac returned. "Blond with blue eyes is the kiss of death with me."

"We'll keep that in mind," Spence said. "It's time to go home. I've got to get up early tomorrow."

Alex remained silent in the truck after she and Tuck left the restaurant. She debated her decision back and forth, changing her mind every time.

When they reached the condo, she turned to Tuck. "You want to come in for a while?"

To her surprise, Tuck shook his head no. "If I came in, I'm afraid I'd pressure you to let me make love to you. I don't want to do anything to slow down your memory returning."

Alex considered his words. Would it affect her memory? She didn't think so. In fact, it might improve her memory. And, as he had pointed out before, he certainly couldn't get her pregnant.

"You once said you thought it would help me remember."

He snapped his head around to stare at her. "Does that mean you've changed your mind?"

She couldn't bring herself to speak. But a nod of her head seemed enough to make Tuck move. Before she knew it, he was out of his truck and around to her door, swinging it open.

"Come on, sweetheart, let's get inside."

Now that she'd voiced her decision, misgivings filled her. "Do you think we should?"

Tuck braced his arms on the open door and glared at her. "Hell, yes, I think we should! I've been thinking that way for four months!"

She hadn't meant to be a tease. Sliding down from the truck into his arms seemed the easiest way to show her agreement. It wasn't that she didn't want this. She'd been hungry for his lovemaking since her return. She'd been so confused, however, she was afraid to make another mistake.

He scooped her into his arms, kicked his truck door shut, and strode to the front door of the condo. "You got the keys?"

She dug them out of her purse and, from his arms, slid the key into the lock, releasing the door. Once he had her over the threshold, he slid her down his body and covered her lips with his.

Alex was reminded of why she'd thought this was a good idea.

And why she'd feared it.

The strength of their attraction, the desperate need that filled her when he touched her, both exhilarated her and made her fear losing control. Walking away from this man might be impossible if she made love to him too many times.

Even when she couldn't remember them.

Tuck's hands were slipping under her sweater, seeking her skin, leaving hunger in their wake. She wanted to feel his touch on every square inch of her body. She reached for the hem of her sweater and whipped it over her head, tossing it on the floor.

Tuck groaned, she hoped in appreciation for her assistance, even as he continued to kiss her. Then her busy fingers began unbuttoning his shirt, eager to stroke his skin, to measure the expanse of his broad shoulders and well-developed chest.

He was no less enthusiastic in helping her remove

his clothing. He also began moving them toward the stairs. When his lips left hers to caress her neck, he pleaded, "Upstairs, sweetheart. And hurry. I'm too old for the floor, but I can't wait much longer."

Excitement raced through her. "I'll beat you there," she whispered even as she pulled away and hurried up the stairs.

His thundering boots assured her she hadn't left him in her wake. Since his arms snaked around her waist at the top of the stairs and lifted her against him, they arrived at the bed at the same time.

She'd thought she'd be shy about showing her body to Tuck. The changes the baby had made weren't enormous at this point, but they made her self-conscious. But she realized Tuck could erase all doubt from her mind.

When they were stretched out beside each other on the bed, there was no time for examination. Only for the hot, pulsing urge that brought them together. His mouth and hands were driving her to distraction and she tried to return the favor.

When he plunged into her, she was eager for him, urging him closer, deeper, wanting more and more, until she couldn't think anymore, couldn't distinguish between her moans and pleas and his. Couldn't ever want to be separated again.

Couldn't think of anything except the man inside her.

When sanity returned, she feared he would pull away. Sex was over. Time to go home.

Instead he pulled her closer to him again, to cuddle and stroke her, to kiss her shoulder, her neck, her mouth, her forehead, as if committing her to memory.

"Are you all right?" he whispered.

"Yes. Are you?"

He chuckled. "If I can ever walk again, I'll be all right. You are so…so—you make me forget everything. I wanted to go slow, to be careful, because of the baby, but that didn't happen, did it?"

She smiled, pleased with his words. "I don't remember slow," she assured him, "but then I don't remember much. Just love."

He cuddled her closer. "That's all you need to remember. Next time we'll work on slow."

TUCK COULDN'T BELIEVE he was holding her again, loving her again. For four months he'd tried to convince himself that what they had wasn't so special. That he could recover from loving Alex. That a sophisticated lady lawyer couldn't tie him in a knot.

But he was wrong.

This lady could do anything to him she wanted.

Now what? Would she leave him and go back to Dallas? Would she consider staying here, becoming a part of his life, her and the baby? What if it wasn't his baby? He'd tried not to consider that idea.

Not that he believed Alex had left his bed to go back to Lowery's. He couldn't believe that. But she might've been involved with Lowery before they'd met. Before they'd made glorious love with each other.

There was a remote possibility that Lowery was the father of her baby. Very remote. But he wasn't going to give up Alex, even if the baby wasn't his. Her next one would be.

And he could love this child, because it was Alex's.

He stroked her tummy, noticing that her waist was larger, her stomach not as flat. "I see the baby inside you," he whispered, fascinated by the changes.

"I'm going to get very fat."

He smiled at the hint of anxiety in her voice. Leaning over, he kissed her stomach. "No, not fat. Just right. You and the baby will be beautiful together."

"I've heard women get very cranky in their last trimester," she warned.

"Ah. I'll give you back rubs, foot massages and lots of loving. Will that help?"

"Yes," she said, drawing out the word because his stroking was growing more and more sensual. "I might even forget I'm pregnant, the way you touch me."

He grinned. "Sweetheart, that's my intent."

Within minutes they were making love again. This time, as Tuck had promised, they slowed down, enjoying each other's bodies, giving Alex a chance to learn again all about her lover's likes and dislikes. Tuck told her there wasn't anything she could do to him that he'd dislike.

Except leave him again.

Then, almost in an instant, their senses heated up, their touch grew more frantic.

When their sweat-slickened bodies subsided beside each other again, Tuck watched Alex's eyes drift shut. "Was it too much for you? I shouldn't have been so greedy but it's been so long that I—"

She leaned over and kissed him. "I'm not complaining. I wanted it as much as you did."

"So why haven't you opened your eyes?"

"Because I'm tired now. I think I need to go to sleep." Her voice grew more and more indistinct.

Tuck bent over and kissed her stomach again, then stroked it softly with his hand. He thought she'd already gone to sleep when she suddenly jumped and squealed.

"What?" he demanded, fearing he'd hurt her. "What did I do? What's the matter?"

"The baby!"

"I'll call the doctor," he said, moving off the bed with lightning pace.

"No! It moved!"

Tuck froze, staring at her stomach. "Do you think we upset him? I mean, did he know?" He couldn't believe he was blushing, but he could feel his cheeks heat up.

"No, of course not." Alex's voice calmed him and Tuck came back to the bed.

"What does that mean?"

"What? The baby moving? It's a good thing. It means she's probably healthy. I was wondering when I would feel anything."

"That's a good sign?"

"Of course. There it is again," she whispered, awe in her voice as her hand rested on her stomach.

"Can I feel?" he asked, sitting beside her, reaching out his hand.

She took his hand and placed it on her belly, moving it around in a small circle. Suddenly Tuck felt a small flutter. He stared at Alex. "Was that him?"

"Yes! Yes, that was her," she said, laughter lighting up her beautiful face.

"Why do you keep saying she?" he asked.

"I don't know. I've thought of the baby as a girl ever since I heard I was pregnant. Why do you keep saying he?"

Tuck gave her a sheepish look. "It never occurred to me the baby would be anything else. Have you had the test to tell you if it's a boy or a girl?"

"No. I could've had an ultrasound done by now, but—well, I've had too much on my mind."

"I'll call Doc first thing in the morning," Tuck said without thinking. He was brought up short by Alex's response.

"I'll call the doctor when I'm ready to go see him."

"But, Alex, you need—"

"It's my decision, Tuck. After all, we don't know that this baby is yours."

She didn't look any happier than him about that possibility.

"Look, Alex, I don't care—"

"Don't say that!" She pulled away from him.

"What? How do you even know what I was going to say?"

She looked away from him. "You were going to say it didn't matter whose baby it is. Weren't you?"

He stared at her, his hand again stroking her stomach, but the child rested. "So? What's wrong with saying that?"

"It's easy for you to say because you don't really

believe the baby is his. You feel confident it's your baby. Right?''

''Yeah, but I know how I feel.''

''Just…just wait, Tuck. That will be the best ,thing. Let's just wait.''

He wanted to argue with her, but she sounded unbelievably tired. He pulled her into his arms again, cuddling her close. ''Go to sleep, sweetheart. You've got to get your rest. We'll talk about everything later.''

She settled against him, as if they slept like this every night. Tuck hoped they would in the future. Whoever's baby she carried.

He'd wait as long as necessary for her to believe him. But he wouldn't wait on the doctor. Whatever she said, he was calling Doc first thing in the morning.

Chapter Fourteen

He wasn't asleep.

Not really. He was in that dream state on the verge of wakefulness, but not quite there. Which probably explained why he heard the knocking at once.

Jerking awake, he stared at Alex, still sleeping peacefully against him. The knocking sounded again, and he slid his arm from beneath her and got out of bed, trying not to wake her. Grabbing his jeans, he pulled them on and hurried down the stairs, buttoning them as he went.

Yanking open the door so the caller wouldn't knock again, he opened his mouth and then stopped.

His mother stood on the doorstep.

"Mom!"

With her gaze going from his bare feet, bare chest, and sleep-tousled hair back to his face, she replied calmly, "Tuck."

"Uh, I guess it's obvious—um, why are you here?"

"Yes, it's obvious. I'm here to see if Alex wants to ride into Lubbock with me. There are a couple of things we need for the barbecue, and I thought she might enjoy a shopping trip.''

Tuck ran a hand over his face, trying to pull himself together. "I'm going to try to get her in to see Doc this morning, so I don't think she can.''

"Is it anything urgent?" Ruth asked, worry on her face. "I thought she was feeling fine when you two came for dinner.''

"I am fine," Alex said from the stairway, looking beautiful wrapped in a silk robe.

Tuck hurried to her side. "I thought you'd keep sleeping." He wanted to kiss her, but he didn't think she'd want to advertise their intimacy to his mother. Not that she could miss that fact, with both of them in semi-undressed states.

That's when he remembered they'd undressed on their way to the bedroom. Avoiding his mother's gaze, he bent and picked up Alex's sweater and bra and tossed them behind a chair.

Ruth sent him a speculative stare, but said nothing, turning her attention to Alex. "Then why don't you put off the doctor and come with me? I doubt he can get you in on such short notice anyway.''

"I'd love to," Alex said, returning that smile.

"No! I want you to see Doc this morning," Tuck insisted.

"There's no reason—" Alex began.

"I think there is.''

"Maybe if you told me what the problem is, I could vote, too," Ruth said with a smile.

Tuck and Alex exchanged looks. Finally Alex said, "I think maybe we should tell your mother, Tuck. Today or tomorrow, it doesn't matter.''

"But what about my dad? He should be here, too."

Ruth jumped in. "I could call him. He's only five minutes away." Her hopeful expression showed she expected good news.

"Yeah, why don't you call him, Mom, while I put on a pot of coffee. I'll make your tea, too, sweetheart. You go get dressed." This time Tuck didn't hesitate to kiss Alex. The news was going to be out in a few minutes.

Alex pulled from his arms and started up the stairs. Then she leaned back down. "Some toast would be nice, too, Tuck."

"Coming right up."

Ruth had hung up the phone and stared at her son. "You even cook for her? Wow, I'm impressed."

"Toast, Mom. It's not exactly a gourmet meal." He headed for the kitchen and his mother trailed after him.

"Are you going ahead with the kitchen redo?"

"Yeah, Ralph and Alex picked everything out. It's going to take him a couple of months, so we might be showing up at your house for a few meals."

"We?" Ruth asked, again hopefully.

Tuck stared at the ceiling, as if he could actually see Alex upstairs dressing, before looking at his mother. "I hope we. Nothing's settled yet."

"Nothing's settled yet? Then what are you going to tell us? Why is your father coming? I thought—"

"Calm down, Mom," Tuck said, continuing to fix the coffee. "I can't explain until Dad and Alex are here."

Ruth sat at the breakfast table. "I'd hoped you and Alex were going to announce your marriage. I've always dreamed of your wedding."

"I hadn't," Tuck said with a grin. Then, to his mother's pleasure, he added, "Until I met Alex."

The teakettle sang, the doorbell rang and Alex came down the stairs all at once.

Ruth went to the door, Tuck poured the boiling water into a cup, and Alex sat at the kitchen table. By the time Ruth and Frank came into the kitchen, Tuck had poured three cups of coffee for the rest of them.

"Morning, Dad. Sorry to disturb you," Tuck said as he waved to the table for them to be seated. He carried two plates of toast to the table, adding butter and jelly from the refrigerator, and joined them.

"Morning, Alex," Frank said with a smile, then nodded to his son. "Ruth said you needed to talk to us."

Tuck sat beside Alex. After rubbing his chin, he said, "Yeah, we do. But we need your promise that you won't say anything to anyone until tomorrow night."

"At the barbecue?" Ruth asked, her gaze sharpening in question.

"Yeah, at the barbecue. We were supposed to tell you right before the barbecue, but I reckon things will be hectic then, anyway."

"Tell us what?" Frank asked.

"About the babies," Tuck said with a sigh.

Stunned silence filled the room.

Then Ruth, sounding as if she were choking, questioned, "Babies?"

ALEX FELT she should take over the explanation before Tuck gave his mother heart failure. After a couple of sips of her herbal tea, she was feeling more awake.

"Both Jessica and Melanie are expecting," she said. Then, feeling her cheeks heat up, she added, "So am I."

"You're—you're— I'm going to be a grandmother?" Ruth screamed, half standing, then collapsing into her chair.

Frank put his arm around her. "Calm down, Ruth, honey. You're going to make yourself sick."

Alex hated making her next announcement. But it had to be said. "I don't know."

Both the older people on the other side of the table froze. Then Frank leaned forward. "You don't know what?"

"I don't know if you're going to be grandparents." She lifted her chin and stared at a point on the wall behind them. She wouldn't act ashamed of her baby.

Frank turned to Tuck. "What's she mean?"

Tuck slid his arm around her, and Alex appreciated his support. She couldn't keep herself from leaning against him.

"The fact is, until the baby is born, or Alex recovers her memory, we can't be sure the baby is mine. I believe it is, but another man, an attorney Alex worked with, also seems to think—he says the baby is his."

Alex steeled herself for their condemnation. After all, it wasn't a pretty picture.

Ruth reached out and clasped Alex's hand. "You poor dear. How upsetting this must be."

Alex couldn't help sniffing as she caught her breath. "Oh, Ruth, thank you. I—I know this is upsetting for you. I want the baby to be Tuck's, really I do. But I can't remember!"

"Calm down, little lady," Frank cautioned. "Best I remember, pregnant ladies shouldn't get upset. Whoever's baby it is, we want it healthy."

Tears formed in Alex's eyes and she hid her face against Tuck's shoulder. Such kindness in the face of her news was more than she'd expected.

"That's why you want her to go to the doctor? Lordy, Alex, haven't you been to a doctor yet?" Ruth demanded.

Alex pulled back from Tuck, trying to wipe away the moisture surreptitiously. "Yes. I went to a doctor before I had my accident. I'm taking vitamins. But I haven't been back, and that was a couple of months ago." She paused, then added, "We felt the baby move last night."

"Already?" Ruth exclaimed. "Why, that— Wait a minute. How far along are you?"

"The last time we were together was Jess and Cal's wedding," Tuck said.

"Over four months ago?" Ruth figured. Then she looked sharply at her son. "How far along are Jessica and Melanie?"

Tuck cleared his throat. "Um, we figure the same time."

Frank looked at both of them and then said, "Hell, there was a lot of celebratin' that day, wasn't there?"

Tuck grinned in response, and Alex elbowed him in the ribs. "Quit looking so proud of yourself."

"Sweetheart," he said, staring into her eyes, "any man who got to be with you ought to be proud."

She buried her face against him, unable to face his parents and not knowing what to say.

"So, when's the wedding?" Frank asked, as if weddings were common events. Come to think of it, they had been in Cactus lately, Alex reminded herself.

Tuck didn't answer his father's question. Alex raised her head with a sigh. She supposed he wanted her to respond. "I have refused to accept Tuck's proposal until we find out if he's the father of the baby."

Frank frowned. "Excuse me for asking, but do you love him?"

Alec looked down at the table, thinking about last night. She hadn't come to a conscious decision last night because she'd been overwhelmed by Tuck's lovemaking. But she knew. Maybe she'd always known, deep inside her. It was too fast, and they hadn't spent a lot of time together, but she knew.

Looking at Frank, she took her courage in her hands and told the truth. "Yes, I do."

Tuck let out a whoop and pulled her against him, his mouth covering hers. She tried to protest, because his parents were right there, but it took several minutes to convince Tuck to restrain himself.

Then she reminded him of something that had bothered her. "You never said you loved me."

"Are you crazy, woman? I asked you to marry

me, didn't I? Besides, I told you—the night of Cal's
wedding. And you don't remember.''

"You did?" Alex closed her eyes, trying to remember. She wanted that memory to hold close to
her heart. But it wasn't there.

"Sorry, sweetheart, I should've told you," Tuck
said softly, dropping another kiss on her lips.

"Well, that clears things up," Frank said, rubbing
his hands together. "I could probably convince our
justice of the peace to be there tomorrow night for
a wedding ceremony if you wanted it then."

Alex started shaking her head before she could
speak. "I told Tuck I couldn't marry him before I
know whose baby I'm carrying. It just wouldn't be
right."

Ruth leaned forward. "You mean, you love my
son, but you don't intend to marry him if it's not
his baby?" She looked at Alex as if she had a screw
loose. "Why not?"

It would be so easy to let these three convince
her, Alex thought. Now that she'd admitted she
loved Tuck, and he loved her, she would give anything to settle into marriage here in Cactus. She already had her job lined up, working with Mac, and
she'd have family again. And most of all, Tuck's
love.

But it didn't seem fair to Tuck, or her baby, to
take such a step without knowing the truth. She
needed to reclaim her past before she built a future.

"It's difficult to explain," she began, hoping
Ruth and Frank would accept her decision. "I need
to know what was going on when…when everything

happened. I know I was unhappy with my life in Dallas, but—''

''That's why staying in Cactus would be a good idea,'' Tuck hurriedly said. ''I asked Mac to give you a job, you know. I don't expect you to give up law, after all you've achieved.''

She smiled at Tuck. ''I know. He told me.''

''But I asked him not to!'' Tuck said, perturbed by his friend's betrayal. ''I wanted you to think— Of course, I spoiled that plan, didn't I? Anyway, my intention was for you to think the idea was Mac's. I can't believe he broke his word.''

Alex couldn't let Tuck think his friend had done him wrong. ''The only reason he told me was so I wouldn't think he'd betrayed me.''

''What are you talking about? How could Mac—''

''Because we'd already talked about the two of us becoming partners.''

She could tell her words stunned him. He stared at her until pleasure replaced the astonishment. ''You're planning on staying?''

Things were happening too fast. Especially to someone who didn't get enough sleep. She held up a hand. ''I said we talked about it. But I haven't made a decision yet.''

She didn't want to explain her reasons for waiting.

''That would be perfect,'' Ruth said. ''And, of course, I'd be around to pinch-hit when you need to work.''

Somehow, her offer didn't look like much of a sacrifice with that beaming smile on her face.

"Yeah, you'd hate that, wouldn't you, Grandma?" Frank teased, smiling just as broadly.

"But what if the baby isn't Tuck's?" Alex reminded them.

Frank and Ruth looked at each other before Frank spoke. "Alex, if you're Tuck's wife, that baby will be our grandbaby, no matter who the father is, because in the end, Tuck *will* be the father. Just planting the seed doesn't count for much around here. It's the man who tends the seed, who helps it grow, that's the man who will be the father."

IT WAS AN EMOTIONAL morning.

But Tuck couldn't have been more proud of his parents. They were good people. And their warm hearts had brought more tears to Alex's eyes.

Now all he had to do was convince her to marry him.

His mother had gone upstairs with Alex to see her new maternity clothes after calling Dr. Greenfield. Ruth had convinced his nurse, Marybelle, a longtime friend, to squeeze Alex in at ten-thirty.

Ruth had offered to accompany Alex to the doctor, but Tuck had intervened in the conversation. "I'll be going with her, Mom, but thanks, anyway."

Once they were out of hearing, Tuck turned to his father. "You said something about a wedding tomorrow night."

Frank raised one eyebrow. "Yeah. You interested?"

"*I* am. I'm not the problem."

"Are you sure about this, Tuck? If the baby's not yours, will you be able to handle that?"

"I liked the way you put it, Dad. I'll be the father tending to the baby's growth. But more than that, whomever Alex has been involved with, I want to be the last one she's with. I don't want to be without her, if she had a dozen children. That's all I know."

"Good for you, son," Frank said with a smile. "Though, after you've experienced one baby, you might take back that remark about a dozen."

"I doubt it. I'm for having that many, if Alex is willing." And he was. Feeling the baby move last night had brought home to him the existence of the child, a real live person, a joy to share between them. He loved the spring on the ranch, when new babies were abundant. Now he was going to have his own personal spring.

"So, what do you want me to do about my friend, the justice of the peace?"

"Can you explain to him about the situation? I'd like to have everything ready in case I can convince Alex to go ahead. All our friends would be there. It would be perfect."

"Except she wouldn't have a wedding gown. Women are kind of particular about things like that. And flowers."

Tuck cocked his hands on his hips, his usual stance when he was thinking. "I could manage the flowers, but I'm not sure about the wedding dress. She could borrow from Jessica or Melanie, but I think she couldn't fit into them because of the pregnancy."

"If you think they'll keep the secret, you could ask their opinions," Frank said. "Women are good conspirators."

"Yeah. Well, it's a lot of trouble, Dad, and it may not come off. Do you mind?" Tuck rubbed the back of his neck. "I can't promise Alex will cooperate. She's a strong and stubborn woman. She seems to feel it would be dishonest to marry me without knowing about the baby."

"I like that about her." Frank stood and came to pat his son on the shoulder. "And there's no trouble too great for you, son. We're family."

"Yeah, and I'm a lucky son of a gun, too. Alex wasn't as lucky, from what she's said, but once she joins our family, her luck is going to change."

"Yeah. Well, I'd better be on my way, if I'm going to give James a chance to do me a favor," Frank said with a chuckle. "Maybe your mother could handle the flower part. She and Mickey Blankenship were in school together."

"Oh, right. Okay, I'll try to catch her alone. Will it be too much, with the barbecue preparations?"

"Nah. Your mom could've outmaneuvered Napoleon. She'll manage. You tell her I had an errand to run."

His father gave him a bear hug before leaving, and Tuck thought again about how lucky he was in his parents. And what kind of a parent he intended to be.

Ruth and Alex came back down the stairs.

"Where's your father?" Ruth asked, looking around.

"He had an errand to run." Tuck thought frantically, trying to come up with a way to separate his mother and Alex. "Uh, Alex, are you ready to go to the doctor?"

She stared at him. "Is it time already? I thought the appointment was at ten-thirty."

He checked his watch. Damn, they still had a half hour. "Yeah, but I need to run out to the ranch to check on...on a sick horse before we go."

His mother was staring at him in disbelief, but Tuck hoped Alex didn't realize that.

"Okay. I'll go up and get my purse."

"You'll need your prescription for the vitamins you're taking, too," Ruth warned her. "Doc will want to see them."

"Thanks," Alex said with a smile, and started back up the stairs.

Tuck didn't wait. Pulling his mother closer, he said, "We're going to go ahead and plan a wedding for tomorrow night. If Alex doesn't agree, it will be wasted effort, but I don't want to wait."

Ruth's mouth fell open. "That fast?"

"Dad said he could get a justice of the peace to help us. But I need you to arrange for some flowers. I don't want Alex to feel she missed out on anything."

"I'm not sure this is a good idea, son."

"Anything that makes Alex mine is good, Mom. Will you help me?"

"You know I will. I'm so excited about being a grandma, I'd do anything. When are they telling Mabel and Edith?" she asked.

"Not until tomorrow. And remember, you promised."

"I won't forget. And we've still got months yet before we find out who wins."

"You're still thinking about that stupid bet? I'll send you to the spa, Mom. You don't have to—"

"Oh, the prize isn't important, son. It's seeing you happily married and having a family that's behind it." Ruth closed her eyes, as if looking into the future. "It's going to be so wonderful having a grandbaby." She gasped. "The baby will be here for Christmas! I'm going to buy one of those Waterford first Christmas ornaments! And then I'll buy one every year and the baby will—"

"Mom, calm down. Let's take it one year at a time," Tuck said with a chuckle.

"The way things are shaping up right now, I'd better make it one day at a time. Have you planned for a wedding cake?"

Tuck frowned. "Can we get one this fast?"

"We might from a store in Lubbock. I'll go to the florist first, then go on to Lubbock. Anything else we need for the wedding?"

"I don't know. I haven't planned one before, and never plan on doing it again."

"Doing what again?" Alex asked from the bottom of the stairs.

Chapter Fifteen

Alex didn't understand the stricken looks on Tuck and his mother's faces. Had she interrupted a private conversation?

Tuck scratched the back of his head. "I was talking to Mom about redoing the kitchen," he said. "I think it's going to be a real pain."

Alex was immediately distracted. Picking out things for the kitchen had been so much fun. "But it will look great when Ralph is finished, Tuck, really. And it will be so efficient!"

He stepped forward and put his arms around her. "Sweetheart, I'm not changing my mind. But doing without a kitchen for a couple of months could be a problem. I've already told Mom we'll be over for a lot of meals."

Her eyes widened as she realized he was including her. "Uh, Tuck, we haven't— I mean, I don't know when— This is so difficult."

Much to her surprise, Ruth patted her on the shoulder. "Don't pay any attention to the boy. He's always been impatient. You'll know when it feels right."

"Oh, thank you, Ruth, for being so understanding," Alex said with a trembling smile. Ruth's kindness meant so much to her.

But not to Tuck.

"You're not helping, Mom," he said, frustration in his voice.

"Oh, yes, I am," Ruth assured him with a beaming smile. "I'm going to help right now. See you two tomorrow." Before Alex could pull herself from Tuck's embrace, Ruth was out the door.

"What was she talking about?" she asked, puzzled.

"The barbecue, remember? She's going into Lubbock to pick up something for the barbecue."

"Oh, right. Things keep changing so quickly. Do you think it will upset the others that we told your parents early?"

"Nope. And by the way, I liked your announcement that you love me. But I would've preferred to be told last night, when I could respond appropriately."

"What did you have in mind?" she asked, smiling at him, amazed at how comfortable she felt in his arms. Unlike the last few months in Dallas, when her skin seemed to crawl with a crazy itchiness that told her she wasn't comfortable with her life, changes since she'd come to Cactus fit like kid gloves, soothing, rich, beautiful.

"This," he muttered just before his mouth covered hers.

Alex pressed against him, exulting in his touch, his love. She, too, would've preferred knowing his feelings, but then he'd told her in private. But she couldn't remember.

"Let's go back upstairs," he muttered, moving her toward the stairs.

"Tuck, we have to go to the doctor." Then she remembered something else. "And you have to see your sick horse. Do we still have time?"

He let her go reluctantly as she looked at her watch. She loved the feeling that he liked to hold her. "What's wrong with your horse, anyway?"

"Uh, he has a cut on his leg, but I think he'll be okay. We'd better go straight to Doc's office."

"Are you sure?" she asked, knowing how concerned he always was when one of his animals was involved. She'd liked that about him when he showed her his horses on her first visit. There had been this quarterhorse that had— "Blue! I remember Blue!" she said, her voice rising in excitement.

"You do? You liked him best, didn't you?" Tuck said with a grin.

"Is he the one that's hurt?"

"No," Tuck hurriedly said, dropped a kiss on her lips and pushed her toward the door. "It's not Blue. We'll have plenty of time after your appointment. Let's go."

"HELLO, MS. LOGAN," Dr. Greenfield said with a smile. "I heard you were back in town, visiting. Ruth didn't indicate exactly what problem you're having, but I'm glad to help you."

Tuck and Alex were sitting in front of Doc's desk, where they'd been waiting for him to join them. Tuck cleared his throat. "Uh, Doc, there's several problems. Alex was in an accident about a month ago and hit her head. She's had amnesia since then, though she's gradually remembering things.''

Doc frowned. ''Any headaches?''

''There were some early on,'' Alex confessed. ''But since I've come back to Cactus, I've felt better.''

''But you've seen a doctor for all of that?'' Doc asked.

''Oh, yes.'' Alex briefly filled him in on her medical history from the accident. ''But...but I'm also pregnant.''

Tuck felt Doc's gaze shift to him and met it head-on. ''I think the baby's mine, but with her amnesia, uh, we can't be sure.''

''Unless something's wrong, you should probably wait until you return to Dallas for another checkup,'' Doc suggested, but his gaze darted back and forth between the two of them, as if he expected something else.

Tuck knew what he had to ask, but it was downright embarrassing. ''Look, Doc, I need to know— I mean, we, er, got carried away last night and— Could we have hurt the baby?''

The man he'd known all his life stared at him, blinking several times. Then he looked at Alex. ''Did you suffer any pain?''

''No. But right after, the baby moved,'' she said, watching him anxiously.

''Was that the first time you felt it move?''

She nodded.

''And how far along are you?''

Again Tuck cleared his throat. "Uh, the same day as Jessica and Melanie."

Doc grinned but didn't say anything about the unlikely circumstance. "I see. Then I'd say your baby is right on schedule. Any other problems?"

"I want you to do one of those pictures so we can know if it's a boy or a girl. I want to start thinking up names now," Tuck said.

Alex didn't say anything, and both Doc and Tuck turned to her.

"Is that what you want, Ms. Logan?"

"Please, call me Alex. I'd like the sonogram, yes, Doctor, and I'm thinking of staying in Cactus, so you would be my delivery doctor."

Tuck watched as Doc leaned over and spoke into his intercom, asking Marybelle to prepare for an ultrasound. Feeling everything was under way, Tuck relaxed against his chair.

"Actually, I won't be your delivery doctor," Doc said with a smile.

Tuck straightened in his chair. "Why not? Why wouldn't you be?" he demanded.

"You're the first to hear, but I'm taking on a partner," Dr. Greenfield said, looking very happy about his news. "It was just decided this morning. She won't be here for a couple of months, and, if you stay, I'll keep track of your pregnancy until she arrives, but my partner will be the one to deliver the baby."

"A woman doctor?" Alex asked, a pleased look on her face.

He nodded. "She's good, and just gave birth to her own baby a couple of months ago, so she'll be able to speak from experience, something I'll never be able to do, thank God," he said with a laugh.

Tuck frowned. "Are you retiring, Doc?"

"Nope, just slowing down. I'm going to relax and enjoy life. I've been thinking of it for some time, but it's not easy to get a young doctor to move to a small town."

Marybelle opened the office door and nodded, and Doc stood. "Let's go look at this baby, okay?"

Tuck followed Alex into the examining room, but Doc touched his arm.

"Tuck and I are going to go get some pamphlets while you get ready," he said, then motioned for Tuck to follow him.

"Pamphlets?" Tuck asked, looking over his shoulder at Alex as Marybelle closed the door. "There's not anything wrong, is there, Doc?"

"Not that I can tell, but I reckon you need to read up on the finer points of being a daddy. Is there someone else in the picture?"

"A lawyer in Dallas. He claims the baby is his, but I don't believe him."

"What if he's right?"

"Doesn't matter. Alex is mine. I love her and I'll love her baby. That's all there is to it." He stared at Doc, daring him to contradict his words.

"Good for you," Doc said, patting him on the shoulder. "Now, let's see if your lady is ready."

When they went back into the examining room, Alex was lying on the table, a paper garment spread over her body with a slit in the middle of it.

Doc directed him to the head of the table. "You

go hold her hand so she won't be nervous," he added.

Tuck took Alex's cold hand in his, but he wasn't sure who was going to comfort whom. Suddenly he had butterflies in his stomach. "You okay?" he whispered.

She looked up at him, her fingers tightening on his. "Yes, but…but what if there's something wrong?"

He didn't know. He didn't even know enough to understand what could be wrong. "We'll face it together," he promised her.

"Quit worrying, you two," Doc said gruffly. He prepped the hand-held examining tool and Marybelle spread gel on Alex's stomach.

"She hasn't gotten very big, Doc," Tuck said nervously, his gaze darting from Alex's stomach to her face and back again. "Does the baby have enough room?"

"More than enough. And when it wants more, it just pushes its way around. You go home and read all those pamphlets."

"I will," Tuck promised as solemnly as if he were making a vow.

"Now, I want you to watch this monitor," Doc said, pointing to the machine Marybelle had rolled closer to the table. He rubbed the connected tool over her stomach, pressing down on her soft skin.

Tuck watched as a pulsating object came into view, something that vaguely resembled a baby. He leaned closer, then realized Alex was trying to raise her head to see, too. Placing an arm around her shoulders, he supported her.

"That's the baby?" she asked softly, staring at the monitor.

"Yep, that's your baby," Doc agreed. "And you both want to know the sex?"

Tuck swallowed. He looked at Alex, and she nodded. "Yeah, Doc, we both want to know."

"Looks to me like a little girl. What do you say, Marybelle?"

The nurse, who'd scarcely spoken before, nodded. "Yes, a little girl."

"She's better at reading them than me," Doc confessed. "But when both of us agree, we've never been wrong."

Tuck stared at the constantly writhing image, wondering how they could possibly make sense of it. Possibly it was because he was overwhelmed by the sight. His baby. A little girl.

He leaned over and kissed Alex briefly, picturing a baby with golden hair like her mother. "A little girl," he murmured, awe in his voice.

"Are you disappointed?" Alex asked.

His gaze left the monitor and flew to her face, seeing the concern there. "Never, in a million years. I'll only be disappointed if she looks like me instead of you," he assured her with a smile.

"In my experience," Doc said, smiling at Alex, "men form a special bond with their daughters. 'Course, they spoil them rotten, but that's what mothers are for, to keep things under control."

After they left the doctor's office, holding hands, dreaming of little girls and blond curls, Tuck took Alex to The Last Roundup to have lunch. Jessica wasn't there. She'd been training a manager so she'd have more time at home when her baby was born.

They slid into a booth, both on one side because Tuck didn't want a table to separate them. He slid his arm around Alex and pulled her against him after the waitress had left.

"I can't believe that was our baby," he whispered into her hair. "And we have a picture. Mom and Dad are going to be so excited."

"Her first picture," Alex murmured, and he could hear the smile on her face.

He rubbed his hand over her stomach. "I can't wait to see her. I want her to know her daddy loves her."

She didn't respond, growing still under his touch.

"Alex? Is something wrong?"

"I just wish I knew what to do!" she blurted.

He pulled back so he could see her face. "About what?"

"About the baby. About you. About Chad Lowery."

"You can forget about him, that's what you can do," he muttered. "He's a liar."

"You don't know that."

"I can smell it," he assured her.

She gave a weepy laugh. "He wears the most expensive cologne, I can assure you."

"Yeah, 'cause he's trying to cover up that liar's smell."

"Oh, Tuck, I love you so much," she said, still chuckling.

"That's what I want to hear, sweetheart. You just keep saying that, and I'll be happy."

"You've almost convinced me—"

"Mind if I join you?" Mac asked, appearing beside their table.

Tuck was about to tell him to go away. After all, a guy needed some private time with his lady. But Alex pulled away from him and assured Mac of his welcome.

He slid into the other side of the booth. "Have you two been busy today?"

After a quick look, to make sure no one could hear her, Alex told him about the sonogram.

"A little girl? That's terrific. Since the other two are boys, she'll be spoilt rotten," he assured them, a smile on his face.

"She would be anyway," Tuck assured him. "You know Mom is going to go crazy. She's already planning on the Christmas ornaments she'll buy for the next ten years."

"You've already told them?" Mac asked, raising his eyebrows.

"Well, um, the timing seemed appropriate somehow. Mom knocked on Alex's door at nine this morning." Tuck didn't say anything else and Mac stared at him.

Finally he asked, "Is nine o'clock significant, somehow?"

Alex said softly, "My guest from the previous evening hadn't left yet. And…and he wasn't exactly fully dressed when he opened the door." Though her cheeks were red, she was smiling.

"Aha. And I'm guessing his identity is the same as your companion."

"Yes, I'm afraid so," she returned.

"Wait a minute, what do you mean 'afraid'? You weren't complaining last night," Tuck assured her.

"No, I wasn't then, and I'm not now," she assured him.

He rewarded her with a kiss.

"So, does this mean you two are getting married?" Mac asked, smiling at them.

Tuck felt his stomach twist as he read the answer on Alex's face.

"No, not yet," she whispered.

"But, Alex, you just said—"

"I know, and I shouldn't have. It just doesn't seem right to get married before I know for sure what…what I was doing. If I was, uh, having relations with both of you at the same time, why would you even want to marry me?"

Mac started to stand. "Maybe I should leave you two—"

"No!" Alex insisted. "Sorry, Mac. We'll change the subject, I promise. No more emotional tirades."

Tuck didn't agree with her, but he also didn't want to upset her. She seemed to be getting more and more tense.

When their food was brought to the table, however, she seemed hungry. He watched her eat her food and drink her milk, scarcely able to take his gaze from her.

"By the way," Mac said when a lull fell in the conversation, "I came over to join you because I need to talk to Alex about…about a matter she asked me to handle."

Tuck's gaze sharpened. "What matter?"

"I can't say. Client confidentiality. Could you stop by the office after lunch, Alex?"

"I don't mind if Tuck knows, Mac. I intended to tell him...soon. I asked Mac to negotiate the buyout from my office in Dallas."

"You've decided to stay?" Tuck demanded, excitement filling him. He needed every positive he could get right now.

"No," Alex said abruptly. "I haven't decided that. But I know I don't want to go back to Dallas. I'm sold on small-town life."

"There's no better small town than Cactus. Right, Mac?"

Mac seemed to weigh his answer. "It's certainly my choice."

"What are you not saying?" Tuck asked, not fooled by Mac's bland look.

Mac shook his head no, and Tuck turned to Alex. "What?"

"Tuck, have you thought how awkward it would be for both of us to live in Cactus if things don't work out between us?"

He couldn't believe she'd ask such a stupid question. "Didn't you just tell me that you love me?"

She nodded and started to reply but he held up his hand, stopping her. "And haven't I said I love you?"

She nodded again.

"Then why in the hell would we not be together?"

Alex rubbed her forehead, as if it were aching. "Tuck, if this isn't your baby, you might feel differently."

"Do you think I could deny this baby after feeling her move inside you, seeing her on that machine? Do you really think I'm that cold-hearted?" he demanded, outrage filling him.

"Calm down, Tuck," Mac urged.

"Stay out of this, Mac," Tuck snarled, staring at Alex. Then his heart contracted as soft tears trailed down her pale cheeks. "I'm sorry, sweetheart," he whispered, pulling her against him. "I didn't mean to attack you, but you're driving me crazy with your doubts."

"I, uh, think I'll go wash my hands." Mac left them alone.

"I just want to do what's right," Alex said with a delicate sniff. "I don't want to hurt you. I don't want to have to worry about another man intruding into our lives. I want everything to be perfect," she finished, her voice rising on a wail.

He cuddled her against him, calling himself all kinds of names for pushing her. Doc had warned about avoiding stress, as had her other doctors. And here he was, pushing her again.

"I'm sorry, sweetheart. I shouldn't be pressing you. We'll take our time, okay? You let me know when you're ready."

By the time Mac arrived back at the table, Alex had recovered. "I apologize, Mac. I seem to get weepier since I got pregnant."

"No problem. Say, do you think it will be okay to tell Aunt Florence about everything tonight if she promises not to tell? I'm afraid it's going to take her a little while to overcome her disappointment."

Alex nodded. "I think so."

Tuck agreed just as the waitress brought their lunches.

It wasn't until after they'd eaten for several minutes that Mac remembered the real reason for his eating with them.

"Oh, what I really needed to tell you, Alex, is that the other senior partners have no problem with the offer we made. We should be able to put through the buyout quickly."

"Good, I didn't think they would mind. We weren't exactly on the same page in what we wanted."

"Yeah, but there's a little problem."

Tuck stared at Mac, wondering what else could go wrong.

"What problem?"

"It's that Chad Lowery. He called me after he heard about you selling out. He's screaming about us forcing you to sell, manipulating your emotions, maybe even threatening you. He's insisting on talking to you."

Tuck glared at his friend. "That guy is going to face the worst threats he's ever heard if he doesn't leave Alex alone."

Chapter Sixteen

Mac left the office shortly after lunch. He had nothing pending except Alex's business, and he didn't want to speak to the madman who kept calling. Alex had said she'd call him on Monday.

Besides, he was concerned about Aunt Florence. Lately, she'd seemed a little down. And it was going to be a sad blow to her hopes to hear that the contest was over.

"Aunt Florence?" he called as he came in the back door of their home.

"Here, dear, I'm in the kitchen. What are you doing home at this time of the day?"

"I'm caught up. Thought maybe we could talk." He stared at her as he came into the kitchen, remembering all the times he'd come home from school, dragging his heels, to find Aunt Florence waiting to tell him everything was all right.

"Well, I'm baking pies for tomorrow night, but I suppose I could spare a few minutes. Is something wrong?"

He licked his lips, not sure how to tell her the

news without breaking her heart. "Uh, well, not for me, but I suspect you're going to be upset."

She sat at the table, her hands clasped together. "What is it?" Her expression was solemn, her jaw squared, as if preparing for the worst. She was a strong woman, his aunt. Strong and caring. He hated doing this to her.

"The contest is over, Aunt Florence."

Disappointment momentarily filled her face, but she shook it off. "So, someone's pregnant? Let me guess. I bet it's Jessica."

"You're partly right," Mac said, smiling slightly.

"Not Melanie, too? Oh, I'm so happy for Edith and Mabel."

And she was. He could see it in her face. She was an amazing woman.

"That's not all."

"It's not? But who...you don't mean Alex is pregnant, too? You must be kidding!"

"Nope. You've guessed it all." He reached out to take her hand. "I'm sorry I let you down."

"Don't be silly, Mac, dear, you've never let me down. I'm sorry you haven't found someone to share your life with, that's all. The years I was married to your uncle were the best in my life."

"Maybe we should be trying to marry you off, instead of me," he teased.

"Now you *are* being silly," she returned, rolling her eyes at him. She got up from the table and returned to her pie dough.

Then she turned around and asked, "By the way, who won the contest?"

"We don't know. All three ladies apparently

were, um, well, the events all seem to have occurred on the same day.''

Florence dropped her pie dough unheeded on the kitchen floor. ''You're kidding!''

AFTER LUNCH, Alex went back to the condo to take a nap. As they'd left the restaurant, they'd met Jessica, so Tuck turned around and retraced his steps to The Last Roundup.

When he found Jessica, he asked her sit with him for a few minutes.

''I've got a problem.''

''Only one? You're in good shape,'' she teased.

''It's a major one. Dad suggested a wedding at the barbecue tomorrow night.''

Jessica gasped in surprise. ''And Alex agreed? That's terrific, Tuck!''

Well, they'd gotten to the center of his problem quickly. Tuck grimaced. ''Not exactly.''

''Not exactly? Did she or did she not agree?''

''I haven't mentioned it. It was going to be a surprise.''

''I don't think that's a good idea, Tuck. You remember the doctor said she shouldn't be pressured. If she's not ready—''

''I know. But Mom and Dad are already involved.'' He held up his hand as Jessica started to protest again. ''I know. But I told them it might not happen. That I wasn't going to try to force Alex if she isn't ready.''

''Good.''

''But, Jess, she said she loved me. She's driving

me crazy. We spent last night together. It was incredible.''

"Tuck, you have to be patient.''

"But would it be wrong to just ask her one more time if she wants to get married? If we have everything ready?'' Tuck watched his friend as she considered his words.

"Well, I don't suppose it would hurt to have everything ready. But you mustn't put pressure on her.''

"Okay. Then here's what I need. What can we do about a wedding dress? Even if she agreed, she wouldn't want to marry in her jeans.''

Jessica made a face at him. "Of course not! Think of the embarrassment when she pulls out her wedding pictures.''

"Pictures! I forgot about a photographer.''

"I suspect there are a lot of things you've forgotten. Let's make a list.''

ALEX LAY on the bed, unable to sleep. She kept going over the day in her mind. And last night.

She loved Tuck. She had no doubt of that now. There was a connection there she'd never felt before in her life. A peace with exhilaration. A feeling that she never wanted to leave him.

She loved him so much, in fact, that she wanted to be sure everything was perfect for him. That he would be father to his child and no one else's.

But she would always treasure the memory of his face as he told her that having felt the baby move, having seen her picture at the doctor's, he could never deny the child. Those words were sweet.

Did she trust him? That question was easy. She'd
trust him with her life. The answer was automatic,
yet it gave her pause. If she would trust him with
her life, would she trust him with her child's life?

No question.

And if she trusted him with her child's life, then
marriage, when she knew it would make her deliri-
ously happy, should be the next step.

Would it be fair to Tuck?

She chuckled as she imagined his response.

With a smile on her lips, she snuggled under the
blanket and began to plan her wedding. As a little
girl, she'd dreamed of her Barbie doll wedding, fo-
cusing on her gown, her hairdo, her bouquet. The
man at the end of the aisle had been a prop of little
importance.

Now she knew who waited for her at the altar
was the most important item in a wedding. And the
man who would welcome her with open arms was
special.

Very special.

She'd worried that marrying him without knowing would harm him. She didn't want to do that. But
after what he'd said today, she wondered if *not* marrying him might harm him more. He would think
she didn't trust him.

Or was she looking for excuses to do what she
wanted to do? Belong to Tuck. She'd wanted him
to come back to the condo this afternoon, to make
love to her again. Could she stay in Cactus for five
more months, waiting for her daughter to make her
appearance, and keep her distance from Tuck?

No.

Even if the baby was Chad's—and, like Tuck, she was beginning to believe that was an impossibility— she knew she didn't love the man. Never would. She loved Tuck with all her heart. He was the only man in the world for her.

If she stayed here and continued to have sex with him but not marry him, there would be all kinds of whispers. Ruth would be embarrassed. So would she. And she'd be denying herself the happiness she so longed for.

She lay there debating the issue over and over again. Until she finally admitted to herself that she wanted to marry Tuck as soon as possible. Immediately, as if an answer had come from above, peace and happiness filled her.

With a wondering smile, she lay there, basking in the fulfillment of her dreams. She was going to marry Tuck. She would be Mrs. Tuck Langford. Giggling like a schoolgirl, she imagined Tuck's face when she told him.

She wished the wedding could be tomorrow. She wished— Suddenly she remembered Frank offering to make arrangements. Could he do that? Was he joking?

Alex sat upright on the bed, her mind racing. Would Tuck approve? She thought he would. After all, he'd been urging her to agree to marry him, the sooner the better.

Another thought occurred. What fun it would be if for once she caught Tuck by surprise. Could she do it?

Not without help.

She grabbed the phone.

BY FRIDAY NIGHT, the phone lines in Cactus, Texas, were into overload. The four best friends who had initiated all the changes in their lives had a lot to talk about.

"I think we've got everything under control," Ruth assured Mabel. "My biggest problem is remembering who's supposed to know what. With Tuck thinking he's surprising Alex, and Alex thinking she's surprising Tuck, it's easy to get confused."

"I think this is going to be the best wedding of all," Mabel said generously. "And, best of all, we'll have three of them married. Now all we have to do is get those grandbabies on the way."

Ruth swallowed and simply agreed. "Yeah."

When she reexplained the setup to Edith, her friend sympathized with her. "My heavens, how do you keep things straight?"

"It's not easy. But at least we only have to do the arrangements once. I talked Mickey into doing the flowers last minute. 'Course, without a church to decorate, it won't be all that much. And I bought a pretty wedding cake in Lubbock and two more sheet cakes to serve everyone."

"Mercy, do you have a place to hide those cakes?"

Ruth giggled. "I've got them on a clean sheet on the bed in the guest bedroom."

"Now, tell me what you need me to do. Shall I pick up the flowers?"

"Oh, would you, Edith? That would help. I'll be so busy here, I wasn't sure how I'd manage."

"Of course I will. My, we've done a good job, haven't we? Except for Mac. Poor Florence." After a brief silence, she added, "Of course, until we get babies, the race isn't over. Florence could surprise us."

"Yes," Ruth said, hoping she could keep the excitement out of her voice.

Florence immediately agreed to sing for the wedding. "I'll bring my tape player, Ruth."

"You're a wonderful friend, Florence. I'm sorry Mac—"

"Don't think a thing about it. Anyway, I haven't given up finding a lady for him. I just won't win a trip to the spa."

"You look better than the rest of us, anyway," Ruth said.

"Flattery will get you anything," Florence assured her with a laugh.

But Ruth knew her friend was hurting. Only there wasn't anything to be done about it right now. But after she got her son married, she was going to put all her efforts into helping Florence find a good girl for her Mac.

JESSICA PICKED Melanie up Saturday morning. As they set out for the condo, Melanie said, "I hope I can keep everything straight. Tuck called this morning to see if Spence would bring his suit."

"I know. But I think he's about decided to accept that the wedding won't happen. He's worried about pushing Alex."

"What changed her mind?"

"I'm not sure exactly. When she called me to ask what I thought about a surprise wedding half an hour after I'd been planning one with Tuck, I was so astounded, I didn't ask any questions.''

''I'm so happy everything's worked out for them. And it's going to be a beautiful evening for a wedding.''

''And a bonfire,'' Jessica added. ''Really big candles, huh?'' Both ladies laughed.

When they reached the condo, they discovered Alex already had cups of tea ready and some bagels she'd bought at the local grocery store.

''Thanks for coming,'' Alex said as she opened the door. ''I'm so nervous I feel like I have morning sickness.''

Melanie groaned. ''Don't even mention those words. The first three months I couldn't keep anything down.''

''Well, at least I didn't have that problem, until now,'' Alex said.

They all sat around the kitchen table.

''Did you talk to Frank?'' Alex asked first. ''Was it too late when you called him yesterday?''

''No, he said he'd take care of the license and the justice of the peace. I made a list.'' She pulled out the list she'd written yesterday when she'd planned with Tuck.

''The florist has promised to make you a bouquet, and, if you want, he can make smaller ones for me and Melanie to be your attendants.''

Alex's face brightened. ''Would you? You wouldn't mind?''

''Don't be silly. Get to dress up and have everyone watching us? Until you appear on the scene, of course," Jessica added with a laugh. "We'd love it."

"Besides," Melanie said, "we want to celebrate with you. We're so happy for you and Tuck."

Alex hugged herself. "I hope Tuck will be happy with what I'm doing."

"You can be sure Tuck will be thrilled," Jessica said with a laugh.

"You're sure?" Alex asked. "I mean, he asked me to marry him, but what if he's changed his mind?"

Jessica and Melanie burst into laughter.

"Oh, Alex," Melanie said as soon as she could control her laughter, "that's one thing you don't have to worry about."

"Let's go upstairs and try on my wedding dress," Jessica suggested. "It's high-waisted, so I don't think you'll have any trouble fitting into it."

"And I brought my white silk shoes. Jessica said you wore a size seven?"

"That's right."

"And I hate both of you. I wear a size nine," Jessica complained.

They both assured her Cal didn't mind her big feet. Then they laughed.

The next hour was girl time, with a lot of laughter and teasing. The wedding gown fit well, though it was a little long.

"Put on my shoes," Melanie directed. "I think my heels are higher than Jessica's were."

To Alex's relief, Melanie was right. "Oh, I can't thank you both enough."

"We're enjoying it, too," Jessica assured her.

"Now, let's check the list. Oh, I talked to the jeweler. He's got some lovely plain gold bands for both of you. Cal is going to pick them up because the jeweler is on the square."

"And he'll keep it a secret?" Alex asked anxiously.

"Definitely."

"Did you talk to Ruth? I'm afraid to call her. What if Tuck is there?"

"I talked to her. She's taking care of the music. Florence will sing. And she said she'd make sure Tuck had a clean suit."

Alex felt laughter bubbling up in her. "It might be hard to explain to the baby if she saw our wedding pictures and her daddy was wearing blue jeans."

"Oh, and Mickey, the florist, is going to take pictures. He'll do a good job, and there wasn't enough time to get a professional," Jessica added.

"Spence's dad is going to make a video for you. He got a new camera recently," Melanie said.

"You've thought of everything."

"Almost," Jessica said cheerfully. "Now, here are the dresses we're going to wear. We both had blue dresses." She held up two hangers with their dresses on them. "What do you think?"

"Blue's my favorite color. Did you tell the florist?"

"We did," Jessica assured her. "Now, it's time for our trip to the beauty shop. Hairdos, manicures and pedicures all around."

THE LONGER THE DAY went on, the more certain Tuck was that he was making a mistake.

Not about marrying Alex. Never that. He knew that she was the woman for him. But expecting her to put aside her difficulties to meet his schedule was wrong.

He would be forcing her, stressing her.

It was wrong.

At least he'd figured out what had been bothering her. Bill had been right. She was unhappy with her job in Dallas. He still wasn't sure why she hadn't told him about the baby, but he suspected it, too, was connected to her unhappiness. After all, what he offered her didn't even begin to resemble her life in Dallas.

Besides, she loved him. That erased every question. And had led him to mistakenly prepare for a wedding. He should call everything off.

The relief that filled him at his decision told him he was doing the right thing. He wanted Alex as his wife, but not until she was ready. "Mom, we're going to have to call off the wedding," he said as soon as he caught up with his mother. "I don't want Alex to feel pressured."

"Of course not, dear," Ruth said calmly.

"Thanks, Mom, for understanding. I'm sorry for all the trouble."

"Don't worry about it," she assured him, smiling serenely.

He said the same thing to his father, thanking him for all his efforts, hoping he wouldn't be disappointed that it was all for naught.

"Son, don't worry about it. We just want you and

Alex to be happy.'' His father continued piling wood on the bonfire.

Tuck lent a hand, stacking logs that some of the ranchhands had cut with chainsaws early this morning. ''I think I'm pushing her too hard. I know you and Mom would prefer that we be married before the baby is born, but that may not happen. But we will be married. We belong together,'' he finished fiercely.

''That's what we think, too.''

''You do?'' Tuck asked, seeking reassurance anywhere he could find it.

''You bet we do.''

''Thanks, Dad,'' Tuck said, squeezing his father's shoulder.

''Nothing to thank me for. Add another couple of logs on that side. It looks a little unbalanced.''

As soon as he finished helping his dad, he'd go call his friends. They'd understand, too. He was a lucky guy.

''MERCY, all this excitement,'' Edith said as she served lunch to her family. Spence and Melanie had come for a late lunch before the two ladies went early to Tuck's to help prepare.

''Sit down, Mom,'' Spence said, grinning at Melanie. ''I think we can add to the excitement, but we don't want you to faint.''

Edith came to an abrupt halt. ''Why would I faint?''

''Because you'll be surprised,'' Spence assured her.

''Come sit down, Edith. I want to hear what

they've got to say," his father said, watching them closely.

Edith took her seat and stared at them, too.

Spence looked at Melanie. "You want to tell them?"

"Yes, please," Melanie said, her smile beaming. "We're going to have a baby."

Edith screamed.

Joe laughed joyously and leaned across the table to pat Spence's shoulder. "Good for you two," he said.

"Oh, oh, oh, I've won! I've won! I can't wait—"

"Uh, Mom, no, you haven't."

Edith stared at her son. "What are you talking about? Of course I won."

"Um, Edith, I'm not the only one who's pregnant."

"You're not? You mean Jessica is pregnant, too?"

"That's right, and she's not the only one."

"But who else—Alex? Alex is pregnant? Oh, mercy."

"Someone had better check the drinking water around here," Joe said with a chuckle.

"But when are each of you due? Who's the most pregnant?"

"I didn't know there were degrees of pregnancy," Joe said.

"Oh, you know what I mean."

Spence cleared his throat. "We hope you'll forgive us, Mom."

"What do you mean? I'm thrilled that you're pregnant."

Melanie spoke softly. "What Spence means is that I was pregnant before we got married. Two months pregnant. We—it was Cal and Jessica's wedding day."

"Oh, my! And Jessica? When—"

"The same day."

"But Alex? Surely she—"

"The same day," Spence informed his mother. "So, we still don't know who will win the bet. But at least you're in the running."

Edith stared at him in astonishment.

ALEX TRIED TO REST. Jessica and Melanie had insisted she should nap this afternoon and steer clear of Tuck's ranch.

"It will be crazy out there, getting ready for the barbecue," Jessica said. "Besides, I'm afraid you wouldn't keep the wedding a secret if you saw Tuck."

Jessica was probably right. She was so excited, so hopeful that Tuck would be pleased, she'd probably spill the beans as soon as she saw him.

Her gaze traveled to the wedding gown hanging on her closet door. It was as beautiful as any of her dreams. Most beautiful of all would be seeing Tuck waiting for her.

She decided to go downstairs and have a glass of milk to calm her nerves. Then she'd come up and change the sheets on the bed. Because tonight, after the wedding, she figured she and Tuck would come back here. For their wedding night.

She couldn't wait.

JESSICA AND CAL went to his parents' house about three that afternoon. Mabel was loading a cardboard box with items for the evening party. "Hi, you two. Come see what I found. Some wedding napkins. They're kind of generic, since we didn't have time to get their names printed on napkins, but I think they look festive."

"Those are great," Jessica said, kissing her mother-in-law's cheek. "Come sit down. We want to talk to you and Ed."

Ed, who'd been watching a baseball game on television, looked up. "What is it?"

Mabel spoke before Jessica could.

"You're pregnant, aren't you?"

Cal stared at her. "How did you know, Mom?"

"I just knew it! I did! I did!" She hugged first Jessica and then her son and then danced around both of them.

Ed laughed. "Don't let her fool you. She's no psychic. She would've guessed you were pregnant if you'd asked her what she thought of the weather. She's been talking about it every day since you got married."

"That's not true, Ed," Mabel protested. Then she grinned at her son and his wife. "Only every other day."

Cal returned her smile. "Well, that's not all we've got to tell you."

Chapter Seventeen

Alex drove her Blazer to Tuck's ranch, her borrowed wedding gown, veil and shoes beneath a white sheet on the back seat. The rest of her necessities was in an overnight bag on the floorboard.

Jessica and Melanie had told her to leave her car unlocked and they would make sure everything made it to an upstairs bedroom without Tuck seeing it.

The baby kept moving, a lot more flutter movements, or maybe that was nerves. She wasn't sure which. It would be such a relief to see Tuck smile when she asked him to marry her.

What if he said he didn't think it was a good idea? What if he'd changed his mind? She knew Melanie and Jessica didn't think that could happen, but—

She parked in the driveway and got out, leaving the car unlocked, tucking the keys in her pocket. Her throat was suddenly dry.

She hurried to the kitchen, the one soon to be dismantled and rebuilt. It suddenly struck her that the new kitchen would be all hers. Such pleasure filled her that she came to a halt, just staring around her.

"Alex? Are you all right?" Ruth asked, hurrying over to her.

"Oh, yes, Ruth, but...but I just realized I planned my own kitchen."

"Why, so you did, dear. Just as Tuck planned."

"You think he knew then that I would—"

Ruth laughed. "Oh, yes, he knew."

Alex took Ruth's hands in hers. "I hope you don't dislike my plan. I wanted to surprise Tuck. Do you think he'll like it?"

"He's going to love it, my dear, just as Frank and I love you. Welcome to the family." Ruth pulled her hands from Alex's hold and hugged her close to her. "I always wanted a daughter. Now I get the perfect one and a granddaughter along with her. You've given us a very precious gift, my dear."

"Oh, Ruth, you and Frank are so wonderful."

"Hey, what's going on in here? Where's my hug?" Tuck's voice had the two women pulling apart. But it was Ruth who answered her son.

"I didn't know you wanted me to hug you, Tucker. Come over here and let me have a go at you."

"Aw, Mom," he said, stepping forward and hugging her. "I was talking to Alex."

"Ah. A mother's life. Discarded for a younger version," she complained, but there was a huge smile on her face.

Alex waited until Tuck stepped back from his mom. Then he swept her into his arms, and she felt as if she'd come home. Before she could speak, which was just as well, since she wasn't sure she wouldn't propose to him at once, his lips covered hers.

She forgot the audience of women, Jessica, Melanie, Ruth and her friends. She forgot about the baby she carried. She forgot about all her problems. There was only Tuck.

A moment later he whispered, "Think we could go upstairs for a while? I missed you last night."

"Tuck, ssh! Everyone will here you," she whispered back.

"I'm so hungry for you, I don't think I care."

"Later. We can go back to the condo later."

"Yeah, later."

They both smiled ridiculous silly smiles that had everyone in the room smiling with them.

WHEN TO BROACH the subject of marriage had been a hotly discussed topic. All the women had different opinions. Finally, it was decided that after dinner, before dessert was served, Alex should take Tuck aside and suggest the marriage.

The wording of the request was left up to Alex, though there had been several ridiculous suggestions.

Alex tried to eat her steak. It was terrific. But she scarcely noticed as she chewed each bite. Her gaze kept going back to Tuck.

He sat beside her, showing no more interest in his steak than she did. And he kept looking at her out of the corner of his eye.

"Did you like the way the lady did my hair today?'' she finally asked, desperate for some conversation.

"It's beautiful. You're beautiful." He leaned closer and whispered in her ear, "Our daughter is going to be beautiful."

"Oh, Tuck," she said with a sigh, and responded when he kissed her.

"Enough of that kissy-face, you two," Cal called from across the table.

"Easy for you to say," Tuck muttered.

Alex felt guilty. She knew Tuck was referring to the fact that she'd refused to let him stay last night. She'd been afraid she'd tell him her plans if he had.

Tuck went back to eating his steak, and Alex pushed the food around her plate. She couldn't eat any more.

Suddenly she realized exactly how she wanted to ask Tuck to marry her. She'd debated several approaches. But the perfect one had popped into her head.

"Uh, Jessica, Melanie, I'm going inside for a minute, if you'd like to join me." She tried to keep her voice calm, her face expressionless, but she felt as though her tummy was full of Mexican jumping beans.

Jessica looked first at her, then Melanie. Then back at her. "Okay. I need to check on...on the, uh, the bread. I think we might be running out."

"I'll help, too," Melanie agreed at once, getting up, but her eyes were wide with questions.

"We'll be back in a few minutes," Alex added as Tuck stared at her. Then she hurried to the house, her friends following.

"What was that all about?" Spence asked.

Tuck didn't know, but he was worried. "You don't think Alex felt sick, do you? She seemed a little pale."

"I don't think so," Cal responded. "Are you sure you don't want to ask her?"

"I can't. I've canceled everything. I think I was acting like an oaf when I decided to spring a wedding on her. It was a bad idea."

Mac leaned toward Tuck. "I don't think asking again would hurt, Tuck."

"I told you I already canceled everything. I want my wife to come to me willingly. And Alex is worth however long a wait there is."

"Hear, hear," said Spence, holding up his glass in a salute. They all clinked glasses and then found another topic of conversation. Baseball. They were a lot more comfortable with that than undying love.

But Tuck knew what filled his heart.

After fifteen minutes he was wondering if he should go to the house to be sure Alex was all right. Just as he decided he definitely should check on her, Melanie and Jessica appeared beside the table.

"Tuck? Alex wanted to see you. She's upstairs in the guest bedroom."

"Is she all right? She was sick, wasn't she? Everything was too much for her. I shouldn't have planned the barbecue. What was I thinking?" he asked himself as he began running to the house.

He never saw the brilliant smiles on the ladies' faces as they pulled their husbands and Mac to their feet and herded them into the house.

ALEX HEARD the heavy boots as they thudded up the stairs. She hoped someone remembered to polish Tuck's dress shoes.

Not that it mattered. She didn't care if he wore boots to his wedding. The only important thing was that he wanted to be there.

A knock on the door stopped her wandering thoughts. "Come in."

She tried to look serene and bridal, smoothing down the skirt of Jessica's gown. Putting on her wedding finery should tell Tuck what she wanted faster than any words.

He stepped into the bedroom, flicking on the light as he did. Then he came to an abrupt halt. "Dear God!" he said with a gasp. "Alex? You're...you're beautiful. I've never seen anyone so beautiful."

"Or willing," she whispered. "I want to marry you, Tuck, here, tonight, if...if you don't mind."

Instead of agreement, she was hurt to see anger on his face.

"I'm going to kill someone. Which one of them told you?"

"What are you talking about? Don't...don't you want to marry me?" She felt her eyes fill with tears and fought to keep them from falling.

"Of course I want to marry you! But I've changed my mind. I didn't want to force you. I know I'd planned the wedding for tonight, but you don't have to go through with it, Alex, I promise. I'll wait. I'll wait forever if it's necessary. I want you to be sure."

"*You* planned the wedding?"

Tuck stared at her, his mind centered on his explanation, his heart centered on Alex. She looked like an angel, a sexy angel, and he didn't think he could take such torture much longer. "Yeah. But I called it off."

"Tuck, *I* planned the wedding."

"No, you didn't, sweetheart, but it's okay. I understand why you want to wait. It's all right." He couldn't take his eyes off her.

"Tucker Langford!" she shouted. "*I* planned the wedding. I don't want to wait. If you want to marry me, I'm ready."

He took a step closer to her. "Why? Why did you change your mind?"

"Because I love you. Because no one could be a better daddy to my baby than you. Because I trust you." She reached out and cupped his cheek. "I trust you to be the best daddy and husband in the world."

"Aw, sweetheart," he muttered, and pulled her into his arms.

"So are we going to have a wedding?" she whispered.

He leaned back. "I want to, but I canceled everything."

"I didn't," she insisted. "Jessica and Melanie rounded up everyone to—" She stopped and stared at him. "Who did you tell to cancel everything?"

"Everyone. Some things had already been done, of course. Jessica arranged for the bands, plain gold. I hope you don't mind. And Mom—"

"Arranged for the music and Florence to sing."

Tuck took up the story from her. "And Dad contacted his friend—"

"And your mom got the cake in Lubbock—"

"And I think we've been had," Tuck said with a grin. "But you know what? I don't care as long as we get married."

"Me, too."

HALF AN HOUR LATER, an aisle had been cleared between the tables, the justice of the peace was standing facing the crowd, his back to the bonfire, but not too close. Florence began singing with beautiful music in the background, and Tuck and his three friends walked to stand beside the magistrate, all dressed in nice suits.

Then the wedding march began and first Melanie and then Jessica walked through the spring night in blue dresses, carrying small pink bouquets.

The music changed. Everyone stood, and Frank, with a beautiful bride on his arm, stepped off the back porch. He led Alex to the front of the crowd, a beaming smile on his face.

Alex couldn't have imagined a more beautiful scene. The fire flickering in the background, a golden moon just rising in the east, spring breezes lifting her veil slightly, and Tuck waiting for her, both of them surrounded by their friends.

When she took his hand, hers was trembling. But so was his. They turned to face Frank's friend, ready to take their vows.

Each solemnly promised to love and cherish each other. Alex was so glad she'd realized how much she trusted Tuck. She prayed the baby was his, but she knew, without any doubts, that he would be the baby's father in every way possible.

They smiled at each other when the man reached the point where he asked if anyone felt the marriage should not go forward.

Until there was a shout from the back of the crowd.

"You can't do this!"

Tuck spun around, outrage on his face.

Alex didn't have to look. She recognized the voice.

The magistrate looked at them. "Uh, this has never happened before."

"Just go on with the service," Tuck ordered.

Even as he spoke, Chad Lowery was coming toward them, still shouting.

"I don't think—" the man began.

"Your Honor, will it affect the legality of our marriage if we take a quick break?" Alex asked.

"No, of course not. If you can resolve this difficulty—"

"Oh, I'll resolve it, all right," Tuck muttered, turning to face the man.

"We'll help," Cal assured him, all three of the other men stepping forward.

Chad Lowery backed up after taking a look at the four men.

They were an impressive sight, Alex thought. She smiled. She should've been upset, of course. But she'd made her choice. And she was happy with it.

She reached out and put a hand on Tuck's arm. "Will you trust me to handle Chad?"

Tuck frowned at her. "Can you?"

"Yes. You can come with me, but I'll send him away."

Tuck looked at Lowery, then her. Finally, he turned to the magistrate. "We'll be right back. Don't forget where you were."

He took Alex's arm and led her down the aisle toward Lowery, who was now backing up.

"In the house, Lowery. We're going to talk," Tuck said with disgust.

Once they were inside, Lowery began to bluster about Tuck forcing Alex to marry him.

She stepped forward. "Be quiet and listen to me, or I'll let Tuck do whatever he wants with you."

Immediately Chad closed his mouth, his fearful gaze on Tuck.

"I haven't recovered my memory, Chad Lowery, but I have come to trust who I am. I don't believe we ever slept together. But whether we did or not, whether this baby is yours or not, I want nothing to do with you. You have no right to interrupt my wedding, and I never want to see you again."

"You can't do this to me. I had plans!" he protested, his voice rising.

"I know. You wanted to be a partner and thought I would be the fastest way. But you were wrong. You won't ride to partnership or wealth on my coattails." She added, feeling a little guilty, "If the baby really is yours, I suppose we can arrange visitations, but—"

"I don't care anything about your damned brat! But you're spoiling all my—"

Tuck struck him before he even knew he was in danger. Then he stood over him as he lay on the floor. "Don't you ever refer to my baby in such a way again."

Lowery pushed himself toward the door, finally getting to his feet when he'd put several feet between him and his enemy. "You're right. I never slept with you. But I was making progress. You were going to let me. I'm sure of it. But I'm glad the baby's not mine. You'll be miserable in this rotten little town, with a cowboy, of all things! You'll regret this day, Alexandra Logan. I know you will!" Then he turned and ran from the house.

They stared at the door, as if the man still stood there.

Finally, Tuck pulled Alex into his arms. "See, I was right. That's my baby girl. I'm her daddy."

"I know," Alex agreed, a beautiful smile on her lips. "Now, let's go get married."

When they reappeared in the backyard, a cheer went up from their friends and neighbors. With beaming smiles, they walked back up the aisle, hand in hand.

"Okay, sir, we're ready to finish the ceremony."

"The, uh, the young man has withdrawn his protest?" the man asked anxiously.

"Either he did or I'm going to have to arrest the groom for murder," Cal murmured with a grin.

The magistrate stared at Cal, his face paling.

"He's joking," Alex said, barely able to control her laughter. "I promise he left all in one piece."

The magistrate cleared his throat. "Very well." And he picked up the ceremony as if there had never been an interruption.

When he reached the part that proclaimed them man and wife, Tuck didn't wait for an invitation to kiss his bride. He pushed back her veil and claimed her lips, forgetting everyone else existed.

Several minutes later Cal clapped him on the shoulder. "Ease up, pal. There isn't a bed nearby."

The magistrate cleared his throat and glared at Cal.

"Sorry, *padre,* but these two have it bad. You have to be blunt to get through to them." Cal grinned as Tuck turned to glare at him. "See, it worked."

"Then I will now present Mr. and Mrs. Tucker Langford to the citizens of Cactus."

Even louder cheers rang into the spring night, cheers that echoed in the hearts of the grinning couple. Tuck held Alex tightly against him and gave thanks that she'd come back to him. Alex lay her head on her husband's shoulder, happiness radiating from her.

The citizens of Cactus gave a collective sigh. They'd never seen such a beautiful sight in their lives.

Epilogue

Ruth retreated to the old-fashioned kitchen with her three friends, even though there were still a lot of people celebrating outside. Not Tuck and Alex, of course. They'd left half an hour ago.

"I'm so happy. And thank you all so much for helping us pull this off. Florence, you've never sung better."

Florence smiled her thanks and started running water to wash the dirty dishes.

Ruth hurried to her side. "None of that, now. I've got help coming tomorrow to do the cleaning. I wanted to thank all three of you, that's all."

"I don't mind," Florence assured her.

"Nonsense. I don't want you to mess up your dress. You might need it for another wedding."

Again Florence smiled, but it was a halfhearted effort.

Mabel stepped to Florence's side and put an arm around her. "Don't feel bad, Florence. We'll all concentrate on Mac now. I bet we can find someone for him."

"I doubt it," Florence said with a heavy sigh.

"Florence Gibbons," Edith began, moving closer. "I've never known you to be a quitter. Just because it's too late to win the bet doesn't mean you can't have a grandchild, too."

"Besides, the three of us want to treat you to the Nieman-Marcus spa. We'll all go together. It will be a great trip."

Florence again tried to smile. "I don't think I'll be much interested in going. But it's sweet of you."

"You'll go, or we won't go," Mabel said firmly. "None of us. But we'll put off the trip until after we get Mac hitched, or it wouldn't be any fun." She hugged Florence close. "And we will find someone for him. Don't ever doubt it."

FLORENCE SANK DOWN on the window seat in her bedroom, staring up at the full moon that had lost its yellow glow as the evening progressed.

All three of her friends had not only found wives for their sons, but they had grandchildren on the way. She was happy for them. Of course she was.

"But, God, why couldn't Mac find someone to love? He's such a good boy. I want him to be happy. And is it too selfish of me to hope for a grandchild? I could never have children of my own. You were good enough to give me Mac. I'm so grateful for him. Truly I am.

"But he was a boy when he came to me. And I love babies. Am I asking too much?" She sniffed as tears ran down her cheeks, and she leaned her head against the window frame. "I know we don't always understand Your ways. But I'm not giving up. I'm going to find a woman to make my Mac happy. A woman who will love him as he deserves.

"You're going to have to stop me, God, if that's not what You want." She sat there, thinking about what she'd said. Then a smile curved her lips. "Maybe You'll decide to help me, after all. I'll take all the help I can get.

"But I'm bound and determined Mac won't be single much longer."

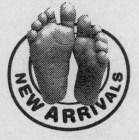

If you enjoyed what you just read,
then we've got an offer you can't resist!

Take 2 bestselling
love stories FREE!

Plus get a FREE surprise gift!

Clip this page and mail it to Harlequin Reader Service®

IN U.S.A.	IN CANADA
3010 Walden Ave.	P.O. Box 609
P.O. Box 1867	Fort Erie, Ontario
Buffalo, N.Y. 14240-1867	L2A 5X3

YES! Please send me 2 free Harlequin American Romance® novels and my free surprise gift. Then send me 4 brand-new novels every month, which I will receive months before they're available in stores. In the U.S.A., bill me at the bargain price of $3.34 plus 25¢ delivery per book and applicable sales tax, if any*. In Canada, bill me at the bargain price of $3.71 plus 25¢ delivery per book and applicable taxes**. That's the complete price and a savings of over 10% off the cover prices—what a great deal! I understand that accepting the 2 free books and gift places me under no obligation ever to buy any books. I can always return a shipment and cancel at any time. Even if I never buy another book from Harlequin, the 2 free books and gift are mine to keep forever. So why not take us up on our invitation. You'll be glad you did!

154 HEN CNEX
354 HEN CNEY

Name	(PLEASE PRINT)	
Address	Apt.#	
City	State/Prov.	Zip/Postal Code

* Terms and prices subject to change without notice. Sales tax applicable in N.Y.
** Canadian residents will be charged applicable provincial taxes and GST.
  All orders subject to approval. Offer limited to one per household.
  ® are registered trademarks of Harlequin Enterprises Limited.

AMER99   ©1998 Harlequin Enterprises Limited

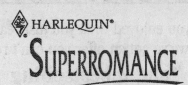

COMING NEXT MONTH

#785 THE LAST STUBBORN COWBOY by Judy Christenberry
4 Tots for 4 Texans
With his friends married and in a family way, Mac Gibbons thought the
bet was over, and he was safe from the matchmaking moms of Cactus,
Texas. That is, until he stopped to help a lady in distress and looked
down into the blue eyes of new doc Samantha Collins...and her baby
daughter. A daughter who looked amazingly just like Mac!

#786 RSVP...BABY by Pamela Browning
The Wedding Party
The last thing Bianca D'Alessandro needed was to be a bridesmaid at a
family wedding. Especially since she'd be bringing a pint-size guest no
one knew about. She could pass off the whispers, but she couldn't avoid
the best man, Neill Bellamy—the father of her secret baby....

#787 THE OVERNIGHT GROOM by Elizabeth Sinclair
Oops! Still Married!
Grant Waverly's career was his mistress...until he found out he
was married! Kathleen Donovan had been his one true love—and
apparently his wife for the past seven years, though neither one knew
it. But now that Grant had a wife, he intended to keep her!

#788 DEPUTY DADDY by Charlotte Maclay
Lawman Johnny Fuentes didn't know what to do with the beautiful
but very pregnant woman with amnesia who was found wandering in
town—except take her home. Trouble was, soon she began believing he
was her husband!

Look us up on-line at: http://www.romance.net